"See something y

The voice made her ~~ ...~~
on the back of her neck stand on end and every
thought fly from her mind. Every thought, except
one.

Leon.

Stop it, she scolded herself. The Prince of Montéz
is French. Of course he's going to sound a little
like him. She really did need to get out more if
that one meaningless episode had the power
to make her lose all grip on reality. She turned
sharply to face him.

And the sight before her almost made her keel
over.

Her imagination hadn't been playing a trick on
her at all. It *was* him. Irritatingly perfect him, his
impressive physique all the more striking in a
formal navy suit. Her mind went into overdrive
as she attempted to make sense of what was
happening. But as she stared at his wry expression
she suddenly understood that this was no
coincidence.

Happy New Year!

This is certainly the year for Harlequin Presents® fans; we have so much to offer you in 2010 that the New Year cheer will just keep on sparkling!

As if the Presents line wasn't already jam-packed full of goodies, we're bringing you more with three fabulous new miniseries! The glamour, the excitement, the intensity just keep getting better.

In January look out for *Powerful Italian, Penniless Housekeeper* by India Grey, the first book in AT HIS SERVICE, the miniseries that features your favourite humble housekeepers swept off their feet by their gorgeous bosses! He'll show her that a woman's work has never been so much fun!

We all love a ruthless marriage bargain, and that's why we're bringing you BRIDE ON APPROVAL. Whether bought, sold, bargained for or bartered, these brides have no choice but to say I do. Be sure not to miss Caitlin Crews's debut book, *Pure Princess, Bartered Bride* in February.

Last but by no means least, we're presenting some devilishly handsome, fiercely driven men who have dragged themselves up from nothing to become some of the richest men in the world. These SELF-MADE MILLIONAIRES are so irresistible they have a miniseries all their own!

January and February see the final two installments of the wonderful ROYAL HOUSE OF KAREDES. But the saga continues in a different setting from April as we introduce four gorgeous, brooding sheikhs with a hint of Karedes about them, in DARK-HEARTED DESERT MEN! Four desert princes, four brilliant stories.

Wow! 2010—this truly is the year of Presents!
Your everyday luxury.

Sabrina Philips
PRINCE OF MONTÉZ, PREGNANT MISTRESS

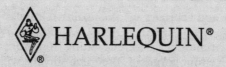

HARLEQUIN®

TORONTO • NEW YORK • LONDON
AMSTERDAM • PARIS • SYDNEY • HAMBURG
STOCKHOLM • ATHENS • TOKYO • MILAN • MADRID
PRAGUE • WARSAW • BUDAPEST • AUCKLAND

Recycling programs
for this product may
not exist in your area.

ISBN-13: 978-0-373-12888-4

PRINCE OF MONTÉZ, PREGNANT MISTRESS

First North American Publication 2010.

All about the author...
Sabrina Philips

SABRINA PHILIPS discovered Harlequin® romances one Saturday afternoon in her early teens at her first job in a charity shop. Sorting through a stack of preloved books, she came across a cover featuring a glamorous heroine and a tall, dark, handsome hero. She started reading under the counter that instant—and has never looked back!

A lover of both reading and writing, Sabrina went on to study English with classical studies at Reading University. She adores all literature but finds there's nothing else *quite* like the indulgent thrill of a romance novel.

After graduating, Sabrina began to write in her spare time, but it wasn't until she attended a course run by author Sharon Kendrick in a pink castle in Scotland that she realized if she wanted to be published badly enough, she had to *make* time. She wrote anywhere and everywhere and thankfully, it all paid off—a decade after reading her very first Harlequin novel, her first submission—*Valenti's One-Month Mistress*—was accepted for publication in 2008. She is absolutely delighted to have become a published author and to have the opportunity to create infuriatingly sexy heroes of her own, she defies both her heroines—and her readers—to resist!

Sabrina continues to live in Guildford with her husband, who first swept her off her feet when they were both sixteen and poring over a copy of *Much Ado About Nothing*. She loves traveling to exotic destinations and spending time with her family. When she isn't writing or doing one of the above, she works as deputy registrar of civil marriages, which she describes as a fantastic source of romantic inspiration and a great deal of fun.

For more information please visit www.sabrinaphilips.com.

With thanks to Penny, for her art expertise
and her much-valued friendship.
And to Phil, whose enduring patience
continues to astound me.

CHAPTER ONE

HER heart was beating so loudly in her chest that Cally Greenway was convinced the whole auction room could hear it. Drawing in a deep breath, she uncrossed then recrossed her legs for the umpteenth time and tried to dismiss it as a flurry of anticipation.

After all, tonight *was* the night she had been waiting for. She looked at her watch. In less than ten minutes, the dream she'd worked so hard for would finally be a reality.

So why did it feel like her whole body was going into meltdown?

Cally closed her eyes and trawled her mind for a legitimate explanation as the penultimate lot, a heavily sought-after Monet, reached astronomical heights. Yes, that was it. She might be a restorer of art, but the art world—epitomised by nights like this, where beauty and expression became about money and possession—left her feeling out of her depth. She didn't belong at Crawford's auction house at the most prestigious art auction in their calendar, she belonged in overalls in her studio.

That was why she couldn't concentrate, she argued inwardly as she tried to encourage the hem of the silky black dress she'd borrowed from her sister back towards her knee. It absolutely, categorically, had nothing to do with the fact that *he* was here.

Cally castigated herself for even having noticed him arrive, let alone entertaining the idea that he had anything to do with the physical symptoms that were assailing her. There was no way any man could have that kind of effect on her, least of all one she'd never met before.

Well, technically. She had seen him once before, when she'd attended the sale preview two days ago, but she hadn't actually *met* him. 'Met' implied that there had been some interaction between them, which of course there hadn't been. He was classically handsome, and the expensive cut of his clothes—along with his very presence at an event like this—suggested he was filthy rich. He probably had some meaningless title like 'duke', or 'count', which altogether added up to him being the kind of man who wouldn't give a woman like her a second glance. Which was absolutely fine, because she had no desire to meet someone that arrogant and conceited anyway. One man like that had been enough to last her a lifetime; she had no desire to meet another.

So why was it she hadn't been able to drive the intensity of his deep blue eyes from her thoughts, ever since she'd walked into that sale room and had seen him standing there like Michelangelo's famous statue come to life? And why was it taking all her willpower not to steal another glance over her shoulder to the second row in the back right-hand corner of the room? Not that she had plotted the layout on an imaginary piece of graph paper and knew his exact co-ordinates, or anything. Why would she? *Because every time you look round he slants you an irresistible, one-sided smile which sends the most extraordinary shiver down your spine?* an unfamiliar and thoroughly unwelcome voice inside her replied, but immediately she silenced it.

'And finally we come to lot fifty. A pair of paintings by the nineteenth-century master Jacques Rénard, entitled *Mon Amour par la Mer* from the estate of the late Hector Wolsey. Whilst the paintings are in need of some specialist restoration in order to return them to their original glory, they are undoubtedly the two most iconic pieces Rénard ever painted.'

Cally drew in a deep breath as the auctioneer's words confirmed that the moment she had been waiting for was finally here. She closed her eyes again, trying to visualise the air travelling up her nostrils and blowing her errant thoughts aside. When she opened them, the wall panel to the right of the bespectacled auctioneer was rotating in a spectacular one-hundred-and-eighty-degree turn to reveal the stunning paintings, and the breath caught in her throat in awe.

She remembered the first time she'd ever seen them, or rather a print of them. Not long after she'd started secondary school, her art teacher, Mrs McLellan, had held them up as an example of how Rénard dared to push the boundaries set by his contemporaries by having a real woman as his subject rather than a goddess. The rest of the class had been lost in a fit of giggles; between the two paintings, Rénard's *Love by the Sea* went from fully clothed to completely naked. But for Cally it had been a defining moment in her life. To her the pictures spoke of beauty and truth, of the two sides of every story—of herself. From that moment on, she had known unequivocally that her future lay in art. A certainty matched only by her horror when she had discovered that the original paintings were shut away on the country estate of a pompous aristocrat getting damp and gathering cigar smoke, rather than being on public display for everyone to enjoy.

Until now. Because now they were owned by Hector Wolsey junior, whose horse-racing habit had caused him to demand that Crawford's auction house sell his late father's paintings immediately, before they'd even had the chance to say 'in-house restoration team'. Which meant the London City Gallery had been frantically trying to raise enough money to buy them, and had been lining up a specialist conservator to undo the years of damage. To Cally's delight, her enthusiasm, impressive CV and her expert knowledge on Rénard had eventually convinced the gallery team that she was the right person for the job. The job she had wanted for as long as she could remember, and the break in her career she desperately needed.

Cally glanced around the room as the bids took off, starting reassuringly with Gina, the gallery's agent, who was seated just along from her. There was a low hubbub of hushed, excited voices in every row of seats. Telephonists packed around the edges of the room were shaking their heads and relaying bids to eager collectors the world over. Within seconds, the bids exceeded the estimate in the sale catalogue, so much so that Cally was tempted to use her own catalogue as a makeshift fan to combat her soaring temperature—but she refrained, partly because she was rooted to her seat in anticipation, and partly in fear that it might inadvertently be taken for a bid. The moment was tense enough.

Unless you were Mr Drop-dead Gorgeous, Cally observed, her pulse reaching an unprecedented pace as she stole another look in his direction and caught him leaning back with a casual expression, his body utterly at ease beneath the blue-grey suit. She could do with a bit of that— composure, that was. Because, whilst she saw Gina raise her hand in between every figure the auctioneer repeated at speed, it did little to ease her nerves. Even if the gallery had promised her it was a dead cert.

But no doubt that was what Wolsley's son said about the races, she thought, caught between recalling the dangers of trusting anything too blindly and willing herself to relax. No, however convinced the gallery team had been that they had secured enough funds, the only time you could truly relax in a situation like this was if you had nothing riding on it—as *he* clearly didn't, she justified to herself. So what was he doing here when he hadn't bid on any of the previous eleven paintings since he'd entered the room at lot thirty-eight? Just as Cally was about to make a list of possibilities in her mind, something happened.

'That's an increase of—wait—ten *million* on the phones,' the auctioneer said uncharacteristically slowly, taking off his glasses in astonishment as he looked from the gallery of telephonists back to the floor. 'That's seventy million against you, madam. Do I have seventy-one?'

The rest of the auction room went ominously still. Cally felt her heart thump madly in her chest and her stomach begin to churn. Who the hell were they bidding against? According to the gallery team every serious collector with their eye on the Rénards should have been sitting in this room. Gina's horrified expression said it all. Cally watched on tenterhooks as she looked discomposedly at the paper-work in her lap. Eventually, Gina inclined her head.

'Seventy-one million,' the auctioneer acknowledged, replacing his spectacles and looking back to the phones.

'Do I have seventy-two? Yes.' He moved his head back and forth like a tennis umpire. 'There, do I have seventy-three?'

Gina gave a single, reluctant nod.

'Any advance on seventy-three?' He looked up to the gallery.

'We have eighty on the phones.'

Eighty?

'Any takers at eighty-one?'

Nothing. Cally squeezed her eyes tightly shut.

'Last chance at eighty-one—no?'

Cally stared helplessly at Gina, who shook her head apologetically.

'Closing then, at eighty million pounds.'

The sound of the hammer, and the auctioneer's cry of 'Sold,' echoed through her body like a seismic tremor.

The London City Gallery had lost the Rénards.

Horror ripped through her gut. The paintings she loved were to be shipped off to God knew where. Her hopes of restoring them were dead, and the door to the career she'd been on the cusp of walking through slammed in her face. The wall panel revolved another one hundred and eighty degrees and the paintings disappeared.

There *was* no such thing as a dead cert. It was over.

As the people began to gather their things and make their way out into the anonymity of the London streets, Cally remained in her chair, staring blindly at the empty wall. She didn't see the way that Mr Drop-dead Gorgeous lingered behind, and barely even noticed Gina's whispered apology as she crept away. She understood; the gallery's funds were not limitless. Even if they could have raised enough retrospectively, they had to weigh up their expenditure against the draw of the public. At a few million over the estimate, the paintings were such a prolific attraction they'd considered them still worthwhile. But almost double? She knew Gina had been taking a risk to go as high as she'd gone.

So, someone else had wanted the Rénards more. Who? The thought snapped her out of her paralysis. Surely whichever gallery it was planned to get someone to restore them? She knew it broke every unwritten rule of auction-room decorum there was, but suddenly finding out was her only hope. Launching herself from her seat, she rushed over to the back of the room where the row of telephonists was filing away.

'Please,' she cried out to the man who had taken the call. 'Tell me who bought the Rénards.'

He stopped and turned to look at her along with several of his colleagues, their faces a mixture of curiosity and censure.

'I do not know, madam. It is strictly confidential between the buyer and the cashier.'

Cally stared at him in desperation.

The telephonist shook his head. 'He said only that he was bidding on behalf of a private collector.'

Cally stumbled backwards and sat down in one of the empty chairs, resting her head in her hands and fighting back her tears. A private collector. The thought made her blood boil. The chances were they would never be seen by anyone again until *he* died of over-excess.

She shook her head. For the first time since David she'd actually dared to believe her life was going somewhere. But her only ticket out had just been torn into a million pieces. Which left her with what? A night in the cheapest London hotel she'd been able to find, and then back to the cramped town house-cum-studio in Cambridge. Another year of sporadic restorations which would barely cover her mortgage, because on the rare occasions a career-altering piece like this came up it only ever seemed to matter who you knew and never what you knew.

'You look like you could use a drink.'

The accented voice was French, and to her surprise it sent an even more disturbing tremor through her body than the sound of the auctioneer's hammer. Perhaps because she knew immediately who the voice belonged to. Though she had told herself that if he came near the alarming effect he had on her would inevitably diminish, the reality was that it seemed to double in strength. She ran her hands through her hair as if she'd really just been fixing it all along and turned around to face him.

'I'm fine, thank you.'

Fine? Cally laughed inwardly at her own words. Even if she'd been asked to restore every painting in the auction she doubted it would have been possible to describe her mental state as 'fine', with all six-foot-two-inches of him stood before her, filling her body with sensations she barely even recognised and which she certainly had no desire to confront.

'I'm not convinced,' he said, looking at her altogether too closely.

'And who are you, Crawford's post-auction psychologist?' Cally replied, unnerved by his scrutiny. 'Brought in during the final ten lots ready to mop up the disappointed punters after the show?'

A wry and thoroughly disarming smile crossed his lips. 'So you did notice me as soon as I walked in.'

'You didn't answer my question,' Cally retorted, colouring.

'So I didn't.'

Cally scowled. There was only one thing she hated more than people who oozed wealth, and that was people who were selective with the truth. She picked up her handbag and zipped it shut.

'Thank you for your concern, but I have to get back to my hotel.' She turned to walk towards the open doors at the back of the room.

'I'm not,' he countered. 'A psychologist, that is.'

She turned, no doubt just as he'd known she would. It was arrogant, but at least it was honest. 'Then who are you?'

'I'm Leon,' he replied, stepping forward and extending his hand.

'And?'

'I'm here in connection with my university.'

So, he was a uni lecturer? Her first and utterly shameful thought was that she should have done her degree in France. The art professors she'd known had all been pushing sixty, and had looked like they hadn't seen a razor, and smelled like they hadn't used a can of deodorant, for just as long. Her second was pure astonishment; he seemed to exude too much wealth and sophistication. But then all Frenchmen were known for being stylish, weren't they? And it did explain why he'd simply been observing, not buying. She castigated herself for being too quick to judge.

'Cally,' she said, extending her hand in return, then wondered what the hell she'd been thinking when the touch of his fingers made her inhale so sharply that speech deserted her.

'And *are* you a disappointed punter?' He raised one eyebrow doubtfully.

'You think I'm not the type?' she rebounded defensively, finding her voice again, though she didn't know why she was arguing with him when as a lecturer he was no more likely to have the spare cash to buy a priceless painting than she was.

'I think you didn't make a single bid.'

'So, you noticed me right back?' Cally replied with more pleasure than she ought to have felt. He hadn't given her a second glance two days ago, when she'd been wearing her usual work clothes instead of dolled up as tonight's occasion demanded. Besides, why should it matter if he had noticed her? It would only be a matter of time before he noticed someone else.

He nodded. 'Indeed. And, since you haven't answered my question about whether or not you are a disappointed punter, it seems we're even.'

She stared at the wall where the paintings had been only moments before and was hit by a renewed sense of failure. 'It's complicated. Let's just say tonight should have changed my life for the better. It didn't.'

'The night is young,' he drawled with a supremely confident grin.

Cally dragged her eyes away from his lips and made a show of looking at her watch, horrified to find that she was almost tempted to find out what he meant. Ten-fifteen. 'Like I said, I have to get back to my hotel.'

She turned to walk towards the door.

'Do you have a better offer waiting at your final destination, or are you just the kind of woman who is scared of saying yes?'

Cally froze, not turning round.

'No. I'm the kind of woman who is well aware that asking someone you've only just met out for a drink is really asking for something else entirely, and I'm not interested.'

Leon whistled through his teeth. 'So you prefer a man to cut to the chase? Detail exactly what he has in mind before you agree?'

She blushed. 'I would prefer it if a drink only meant a *drink.*'

'So you *are* thirsty, *chérie?*'

Cally swallowed, her mouth going inconveniently dry. Was she the kind of woman who was scared of saying yes? she wondered, suddenly both horrified and aggrieved that he might actually be right. No, she justified, she wasn't afraid—she'd just learned from experience that *that* kind of yes inevitably led to disappointment. Which was why— unlike other girls she knew, who invariably spent their evenings making out with random guys in clubs—she'd spent the last seven years sitting at her desk into the early hours of every morning memorising the chemical make- up of conservation treatments, practising each and every technique for the sake of her precious career. But look where it had got her now! Precisely nowhere.

Cally took a deep breath. 'Yes' might very well lead to disappointment, but right now it didn't get much more dis- appointing than the thought of returning to her hotel with nothing but her misery and the overpriced minibar for company. At least accepting the offer of one drink with a perfectly normal man for once in her life would take her mind off what had just happened.

'On one condition, then…' she began confidently, but the instant she raised her eyes she caught sight of his dev- astating smile, and remembered too late that there was ab- solutely nothing remotely normal about the way he made her feel. If anything, that was what she should be afraid of. 'The topic of work is off the agenda.'

'Done,' he answered decisively.

'Right.' Cally's head began to spin. 'Then…where did you have in mind?'

CHAPTER TWO

LEON didn't have anywhere in mind. He hadn't had anything on his mind for two full days—except her. He'd come to Crawford's to view the pre-auction exhibition of the paintings the world wanted to get their hands on, and had found himself wanting to get his hands on something else entirely: the narrow waist and shapely hips of the woman with lustrous red-bronze hair, who'd been transfixed by the paintings he'd suddenly forgotten he'd come here to see. The wave of desire had come out of nowhere, for it was certainly unprovoked. Though the luscious curves of her figure were obvious, she couldn't have been dressed any less provocatively, in a drab, crinkled blouse and olive-green skirt that reached her ankles. He'd wanted to dispose of them both there and then.

And he would have done, if he'd known who she was and that she could be trusted to be discreet. But he hadn't. Standing there, all misty-eyed before the paintings, she'd looked—most inconveniently—like exactly the kind of woman who would cloud everything with emotion and make discretion an impossibility. But the knot of heat in his groin had demanded he find out for certain. How fortuitous, then, that when he'd asked a few discreet questions of his own it turned out that she was the London City Gallery's choice to restore the Rénards. For once in his life, a twist of fate had amused him. She would have to be fully vetted anyway. Suddenly it made perfect sense for him to stay on for the auction and undertake the investigation personally.

Leon watched her as she walked beside him, oblivious to the sound of taxicabs and buses that filled the tepid June evening. To his pleasure, she looked a world away from the olive-green drabness of just over forty-eight hours before; she was luminescent in black silk, the halter neck revealing an ample cleavage, and her striking hair, which had previously been tied back, now fell over her shoulders in waves. Tonight she looked exactly like the sort of woman capable of the kind of short and mutually satisfying affair he had in mind.

'Lady's choice,' he said, realising they had reached the end of the street, and he still hadn't answered her question as to where they were headed.

Cally, whose nerve was evaporating by the second, looked around the street and decided that the sooner this was over the better. 'The next bar we come to will be fine, I'm sure. After all, its only requirement is that it serve drinks, is it not?'

Leon nodded. *'D'accord.'*

As they turned the corner of the street, Cally heard a low, insistent drumbeat and saw a neon sign illuminating darkness: the Road to Nowhere.

'Perfect,' Cally proclaimed defiantly. It might look a little insalubrious, but at least it was too brash and too noisy for there to be any danger of lingering conversation over an intimate table for two.

Leon looked up, to see a young couple tumble out of the

door and begin devouring each other up against the window, and he stifled a grin.

'It looks good to me.'

Cally did a double take, doubting he was serious. Then she wished she hadn't, because the sight of his impossibly handsome face beneath the soft glow of the street lights made her whole body start with that ridiculous tingling again.

'Fabulous. And my hotel is only two streets away,' she said, as much to convince herself that after one drink she could return to the safety of her room as to remind him.

'What could be better?' he drawled, the look in his eyes explicit.

She swallowed down a lump in her throat as they passed the couple, who were yet to come up for air, and entered the bar.

It was dark inside, the sultry vocals of a female singer stirring the air whilst couples absorbed in one another moved slowly together on the dance floor. *Oh yes, great idea, Cally. This is much safer ground than a quiet bar.*

'So what will it be, a Screaming Orgasm or a Pineapple Thrust?'

'I beg your pardon?' Cally swung round and was only partially relieved to see that Leon was reading from a cocktail menu he'd picked up from the bar.

'I'll just have a mineral water, thanks.' Leon raised his eyebrows in disapproval before the words were even out of her mouth. 'OK, fine,' she retracted, briefly running her eyes down the menu. 'I'll have a…Cactus Venom.'

When was the last time she'd had a drink? A glass of wine at her nephew's christening in January. God, she really did need to get out more.

Leon slipped off his jacket and ordered two of the same,

somehow managing, she noticed, to look exactly like he fitted in. She, on the other hand, crossed her arms awkwardly across her chest, feeling horribly overdressed and self-conscious.

'So, don't tell me—you come here all the time.' Cally said, marvelling at how quickly he seemed to have got the waitress's attention, although on second thoughts she could guess why.

'Well, you know, I would, but I live in France. What's your excuse?'

She laughed, relaxing a fraction as they found themselves a table and sat down. 'I live in Cambridge.'

'You mean you didn't know that the Road to Nowhere was waiting just around the next corner?'

'No, I didn't.' Cally shook her head, remembering the auction and thinking that the bar's name was altogether too apt.

Leon seemed to sense her despondency and raised his glass. 'So, what shall we drink to?'

Cally thought for a moment. 'To discovering hard work doesn't pay off in the end, so why bother?'

Something about his company, the atmosphere, made her realise that maybe she did need to talk about it after all. She hoped it was that, and not that she couldn't go five minutes without mentioning work.

'Sorry,' she added, suddenly aware of how discourteous that sounded. 'To…the Road to Nowhere.'

Leon chinked his cocktail glass against hers and they both took a sip of the yellow-green liquid, smarting at the sour taste.

'So, tonight didn't exactly go to plan for you?' Leon ventured.

'You could say that. The London City Gallery promised me the restoration job on the Rénards if they won them. They didn't.'

'Maybe you should offer your services to whoever did.'

'According to the guy manning the phone, it was an anonymous private collector.' Her voice rang with resentment.

'Who's to say a private collector won't commission you to complete the restorations?'

'Experience. Even if I could find out who he or she is, they'll either choose someone they know or the team who can get it done fastest. The rich treat art like a new Ferrari or a penthouse in Dubai—an acquisition to boast about, instead of something everyone deserves to enjoy.'

Leon went very still. 'So if you *were* approached, your morals would stop you from working on them?'

Cally turned away, emotion pricking at the backs of her eyes. 'No, it wouldn't stop me.'

She was aware how unprincipled that sounded—or more accurately how unprincipled that actually *was*—but it wasn't just because of the opportunities that working on them was bound to lead to. It was because she could never turn down the opportunity to work on the paintings that had determined the direction of her entire life, even if that life now seemed to be one big road to nowhere. She shook her head, too mortified to admit as much.

'I'd be a fool to turn it down if I ever got the opportunity. If I worked on the Rénards, I'd be known across the world.'

Leon gave a single nod. So, whatever impression she'd given at the pre-auction, what she wanted was renown. But of course, he thought cynically, what woman didn't? And, going by her protestations that she didn't want to talk about work, followed by her emotional outpouring on the subject, she didn't seem any more capable of sticking to her word than the rest of her sex. Well, there was one way to be sure.

He leaned back in his chair. 'So, was the pre-sale the first time you'd seen *Mon Amour par la Mer?*'

Cally shivered. 'I…I didn't think you'd noticed me that day.'

He waited for her eyes to lift and meet his. 'On the contrary, that was when I decided that I wanted to make love to you. In fact, that was why I came back to the auction.'

Cally gawped in shock at his nerve, whilst at the same time a treacherous thrill zipped up her spine, which surprised her even more than his words. Words which told her that, unbelievably, he had wanted her when she'd been dressed like *Cally,* not just tonight when she felt like she was playing dress-up to fit in with the art world. The world which, contrary to her initial impression, he wasn't a part of either. He who had only been there tonight because of her. How was that possible? Wasn't it obvious that she lacked that sexual gene, or whatever that thing was that most other women had? She didn't know, but suddenly all the reasons she'd amassed for loathing him toppled over, taking her defences with them.

'I ought to walk out of here right now.'

'So walk.'

'I…I haven't finished my drink.'

'And do you always do exactly what you say you are going to do, Cally?'

She was sure he turned up his accent when he said her name on purpose, sure he knew it made her stomach flip. Even surer that she didn't have the strength to walk away.

'I hate people who go back on their word.'

'As do I.' He looked at her sharply. 'However, there were some parts of this agreement we didn't specify—like whether this drink included a dance, for instance?'

Cally drew in a sharp breath as she looked to the grinding mass of bodies on the dance floor, now slowing to a more languorous pace as the soloist with the heavy eye-liner and the husky voice began a rendition of *Black Velvet*.

'You're not serious?'

'Why not? Isn't seizing the moment one of life's beauties that art celebrates?'

Art, Cally thought. It was a celebration of life. But when was the last time she'd actually stopped to remember that and allowed herself to live it? She drank him in—his dark blond hair falling over his forehead, his eyes smouldering with a fire that both terrified and excited her—and for a split second she didn't feel as though she'd lost anything at all tonight.

She offered him her hand and answered him in a voice she didn't recognise as her own. 'You're on.'

As she stood up the alcohol went to her head, and for a second she closed her eyes, breathing deeply. The air felt thick, the heady beat of music vibrating through every cell in her body. She'd loved this song as a teenager. David had hated it. Why had she never played it since?

'Come on.' Leon snaked his hand around her waist and pulled her to him before he had time to consider whether or not this was such a good idea. He wanted her with a hun-griness that unnerved him. He watched her mouthing the words of the song and, unable to drag his eyes away from her full lips, wondered if for once in his life he was going to be incapable of sticking to his own rules.

Always wanting more, he'd leave you longing for...

The lyrics seemed to reach into her soul. *He* seemed to reach into her soul. She had never met anyone like him. She had only known him five minutes and yet—clichéd thought it sounded—it almost felt like he knew her better than she had known herself, about everything she'd been missing out on. Being pressed up against him was intoxicating, the smell of him, the touch of him. She ran her hands up his muscular back, locked them behind his neck and allowed the tension to leave her body as he moved easily, her body following every movement his made.

'Did I tell you how sexy you are?' he whispered in her ear, the warmth of his breath sending an inordinate level of heat flooding through her.

He did this all the time; she was sure he did. Which was why it was crazy. She'd never done anything like this in her life, and she didn't know what she was playing at now. But, though in her head she knew she was probably a fool to continue, right now her body was the only thing she could hear—and it was thrumming with a whole host of new sensations, all clamouring to be explored.

'Did I tell you how sexy *you* are?' she whispered nervously, grateful that she couldn't see his face, hoping he couldn't sense that she was trembling all over.

'No,' he whispered, drawing back to brush his lips just below her ear. 'You most definitely didn't mention that.'

She couldn't bear it. His mouth was playing havoc with the sensitive skin of her neck. She needed to kiss him. Properly. Shakily, she guided his head with her hand until their faces were level, not knowing where her confidence had come from. Had he known if he touched her like that she wouldn't be able to resist him? Probably. But right now she didn't care. She just wanted to kiss him.

His lips brushed hers, painfully slowly, then opened hungrily. He tasted decadent, like dark chocolate and cinnamon. He ran his hand gently down her spine, slowing over the curve of her bottom. It was the kind of kiss that would have been utterly inappropriate in an exclusive little wine bar. To Cally's shock it had a lot more in common with the display of primal need they had witnessed in the street outside, but to her astonishment she wanted more. She told herself it was down to the charge of the music, the distinctive scent of his hypnotic, balmy cologne. But she could blame it on exterior forces all she liked; the truth was that it was kissing *him* that was explosive. Suddenly she forgot everything else—the fact that he was a man she had only just met, the fact that she was bound to disappoint him, that this could only lead to heartache—because her need for him was overwhelming, and he seemed to feel it too.

'You want to get out of here?'

She took a deep breath. 'Yes, I do.'

So, Leon thought, fighting his own desire, there was the concrete proof that her word could not be trusted. That was the rule.

Cally's cheeks were hot and her heart was pounding as he threaded her through the other couples on the dance floor and out onto the pavement, hailing a cab.

He opened the door for her as it rolled up. Then he coolly shut the door behind her and remained standing on the pavement.

She wound down the window, her brows knitted together in bewilderment. 'I thought we were getting out of here?'

His face was grim. 'No, *you* are. One drink was all you wanted, wasn't it, Cally?'

Cally felt a new fire burning in her cheeks as Leon signalled for the driver to go and she suddenly realised what was happening.

'Bastard!' she shouted.

But the driver had already pulled away, and all she could hear was the climax of the song as it poured down the street.

In a flash he was gone. It happened so soon, what could you do?

CHAPTER THREE

As Cally rested her head on the window of the train from King's Cross back to Cambridge, the sky-rise landscape shrinking to a patchwork of green, she gave up sifting her memories for debris and concluded that, no, she had never felt more ashamed than she did right now.

She, Cally Greenway, had almost had a one-night stand with a total stranger.

And, what was worse, a tiny part of her almost wished she had.

No, she argued inwardly, of course she didn't. She just wished he hadn't subjected her to that hideous rejection, or at the very least that she'd been able to understand why he had.

Had the earth-shattering heat of their kiss, which she'd thought was mutual, actually been so one-sided that he'd realised she would be useless in bed? Or was it all part of a game he played to prove that he was so drop-dead gorgeous he could make any woman abandon her morals if he chose?

Cally spent the next week wavering between the two theories, subsequently caught between reawakened insecurities and fresh anger. In the end, frustration with herself for even caring made anger prevail. She should be glad that she'd had a lucky escape, and the reason for his insulting behaviour shouldn't even matter when he was no one to her, a no one whom she was never likely to see ever again.

So why, whenever she thought back to that night, did that moment in the taxi hurt even more than losing the commission had done? Cally pressed her lips together in shame, but then released them. It was simply because up until that point she had thought that what she'd lost was her dream job. He had made her see that she'd spent so long with her eye on that goal alone that she'd sacrificed every other aspect of her life in the process. Yes, she thought, unwilling to dwell on the other broken dreams his rejection had resurrected, that was it. Finding herself devastated that she would never have Leon's arms around her again just proved how long it had been since she'd actually got out there and spent any time in the company of anyone but herself, and occasionally her family.

Well, he might have reinforced her belief about the futility of trusting the opposite sex, but she had to acknowledge that maybe it was about time she accepted the odd invitation to go out now and again, instead of always having a well-rehearsed list of things she had to do instead. Particularly since the short list of restorations she had lined up for the next three months was hardly going to claim all of her time, she thought despondently as she booted up her computer to see whether her inbox heralded any new enquiries on that front today. It was all very well, deciding to get a social life whilst she worked out what to do next, but it was hardly feasible if it meant not being able to eat.

Three new mails. The first was a promotional email from the supplier she used for her art materials, which she deleted without opening, knowing she couldn't afford anything above and beyond her regular order. The second was from her sister Jen, who was back from her family holiday in Florida, desperate to know if the little black dress she'd leant her had been as lucky for Cally as it had been for her when she'd worn it to the journalism awards last month and scooped first prize. Cally shook her head, wondering how her sister managed to pull off being a high-flying career woman as well as a wonderful wife and mother, and resolved to reply with the bad news when she felt a little less like a failure in comparison.

The third email was from a sender with a foreign-sounding name she didn't recognise. She clicked on it warily.

Dear Miss Greenway
Your skills as an art conservator have recently been brought to the attention of the Prince of Montéz. As a result, His Royal Highness wishes to discuss a possible restoration. To be considered, you are required to attend the royal palace in person in three days' time. Your tickets will be couriered to you tomorrow unless you wish to decline this generous offer by return.
Yours faithfully, Boyet Durand
On behalf of His Royal Highness, the Prince of Montéz

Cally blinked at the words before her. Her first reaction was disbelief. Here was an email offering a free trip to a luxurious French island, so why wasn't she pinging it straight off to her junk-mail folder, knowing there was a catch? She read it again. Because it wasn't the usual generic trash: *You've won a holiday to Barbados, to claim just call this number....* This sender knew her name and what she did for a living. It was feasible that someone could have seen one of her few restorations that had ended up in smallish galleries and been inspired to visit her website—but a prince?

She read it a third time, and on this occasion the arrogance of it truly sunk in. If it was real, who on earth did the Prince of Montéz think he was to have his advisor summon her as if she was a takeaway meal he'd decide whether or not he wanted once she arrived?

Cally opened a new tab and typed 'Prince of Montéz' into Wikipedia. The information was irritatingly sparse. It didn't even give his name, only stated that in Montéz the prince was the sovereign ruler, and that the current prince had come into power a year ago when his brother Girard had died in an accident aged just forty-three, leaving behind his young wife, Toria, but no children. Cally cast her mind back, roughly recalling the royal-wedding photos which had graced the cover of every magazine the summer she'd graduated, and hearing the news of his tragic death on the radio in her studio some time last year. But there was no further information about the late prince's brother, the man who thought that she, a lowly artist, could drop everything because he commanded it.

Cally was tempted to reply that, attractive though the offer was, the prince was mistaken if he thought she could fit him into her busy schedule at such short notice. But the truth was he *wasn't* mistaken. Hadn't she only just been wishing she had more work lined up, and thinking she ought to start saying yes to something other than Sunday lunch at her parents' house?

Which was why she decided she would let the tickets come. Not that she really believed they would, until the doorbell rang early the following morning, thankfully interrupting a fervid dream about a Frenchman with a disturbingly familiar face.

Nor did she really believe she'd dare to use them until the day after, when she heard the voice of the pilot asking them to please return their seats to the upright position because they were beginning their descent to the island.

The last and only time Cally had been to France was on a day trip to Le Touquet by ferry whilst she'd been at secondary school, most of which had been spent trawling round a rather uninspiring hypermarket. She'd always fancied Paris—the Eiffel Tower and the galleries, of course—but she'd somehow never got round to taking any kind of holiday at all since uni, nor felt she could justify the unnecessary expense. So when she stepped out of first class and was greeted by the most incredible vista of shimmering azure water and glorious tree-covered mountains sprinkled with terracotta roofs, it was no wonder it felt like this was all happening to someone else. For the first time in years she felt the urge to whip out a sketch pad and get to work on a composition of her own.

A desire that only increased when the private car pulled up to the incredible palace. It almost looked like a painting, she thought as the driver opened the door of the vehicle for her to depart.

'Please follow me, *mademoiselle*. The prince will meet you in *la salle de bal*.'

Cally frowned as he led her through the impressive main archway, trying to remember her GCSE French in order to decipher which room he was referring to. He must have caught her perplexed expression.

'You would say "the ballroom", I think?'

Cally nodded and rolled her eyes to herself as they passed through the courtyard and up a creamy white staircase with a deep red carpet running through the centre. There was a very good reason why she hadn't needed to know the word for ballroom for her project on *'ma maison'*.

The thought reminded her just how hypocritical it was to feel impressed by the palace when the man who lived here was guilty of the excess she loathed. She was even more ashamed to look down at her perfectly functional black jacket and skirt, teamed with a white blouse, and wish she had brought something a little more, well, worthy. Why should she be worried what clothes she was wearing to meet the prince? Just because he had a palace and a title didn't mean she ought to act any differently from the way she would with any potential client. Any more than he should judge her on anything but her ability as a restorer, she thought defiantly, hugging her portfolio to her chest.

'Here we are, Mademoiselle Greenway.'

'Thank you,' Cally whispered as the man signalled for her to enter the ballroom, bowed his head and then swiftly departed.

She entered tentatively, preparing to be blown away by the full impact of the magnificent marble floor, the intricately decorated wall panels and the high, sculpted ceiling that she could see from the doorway. But, as Cally turned into the room, the gasp that broke from her throat was not one of artistic appreciation, it was one of complete astonishment.

The Rénards. Hanging, seemingly innocuously, right in the centre of the opposite wall.

Cally rushed to them to get a closer look, momentarily convinced that they must be reproductions, but a quick appraisal told her immediately that they were not. She felt her heart begin to thud insistently in her chest, though she couldn't accurately name the emotion which caused it. Excitement? She had wanted more than anything to discover the identity of the mysterious telephone-bidder, to have the chance to convince them she was the best person to carry out the restoration. Now it seemed that somehow *he* had found *her*.

Or was it horror? For wasn't this exactly the fate of the paintings she had feared—shut away in some gilded palace never to be looked upon again? She closed her eyes and pressed her hands to her temples, trying to make sense of it, but before she could even begin a voice behind her cut through everything.

'See something you recognise?'

A voice which made her eyes fly open, every hair on the back of her neck stand on end and every thought fly from her mind. Every thought, except one.

Leon.

Stop it, she scolded herself. The Prince of Montéz is French, of course he's going to sound a little like him. God, she really did need to get out more if that one meaningless episode had the power to make her lose all grip on reality every time she heard a man with a French accent. The voice belonged to the Prince of Montéz, who had brought her here as his potential employee, so why was she still staring rudely at the wall? She turned sharply to face him.

The sight before her almost made her keel over.

Her imagination hadn't been playing a trick on her at all. It was him. Irritatingly perfect him, his impressive physique all the more striking in a formal navy suit.

Her mind went into overdrive as she attempted to make sense of what was happening. Leon was a university professor; perhaps he'd been invited here to examine the paintings in more detail; perhaps this was just one of life's unfortunate coincidences?

But as she stared at his wry expression—impatient, as if waiting for her tiny mind to catch up—she suddenly understood that this was no coincidence. Her very first appraisal of him in that sale room in London—rich, heartless, titled—had not been wrong. It was everything else that had been a lie. Good God, was Leon even his real name?

'You bastard.'

For a second his easy expression looked shot through with something darker, but just as quickly it was back.

'So you said last time we met, Cally, but now that you know I am your potential employer I thought you'd be a little more courteous.'

Courteous? Cally felt the bile rise in her throat. 'Well, since I can assure you I am not going to be capable of courtesy towards you any time this century, I think I should leave, don't you?'

Leon gritted his teeth. Yes, he did think she should leave, the same way he'd thought he should in London. But after countless hot, frustrated nights, when all his body had cared about was why the hell he hadn't taken her when he'd had the chance, Leon was through with thinking.

He blocked her exit with his arm.

'At least stay for *one drink*.'

'And why the hell would I want to do that?'

'Because, yet again, you look like you need one.'

Had he brought her here purely to humiliate her further, to revel in how much he had got to her? She fixed a bland expression on her face, determined not to play ball. 'I'll have one on my way back to the airport.'

'You have somewhere else to be?' he replied, mock-earnestly.

She knew exactly what he implied—that she had nowhere else to be today any more than when she had protested the need to return to her hotel room that night. It was the same reason he'd known she would come at short notice. And exactly why staying here could only quadruple the humiliation she already felt.

'No, you're absolutely right, I don't. But anywhere is preferable to being on this dead end of an island with some lying product of French inbreeding who has nothing better to do than to toy with random English women he meets for sport.'

'*Woman*,' he corrected. 'There is certainly only one of you, Cally Greenway.'

'And yet there is one of you in every palace and stately home on the planet. It's so predictable, it's boring.'

'I thought that you liked things to turn out exactly the way you expect them to—or perhaps that is simply what you pretend to want?'

'Like I told you, all I want is to leave.'

'It's a shame your body language says otherwise.'

Cally looked down, pleased to discover that if anything she had stepped further away from him, whilst her arms clutched her portfolio protectively to her chest.

'And do you always take a woman's loathing as a come-on?'

'Only when it's born out of sheer sexual frustration,' he drawled, nodding at the gap between them and her self-protective stance.

'In your dreams.'

'Yours too, I don't doubt.' He looked at her with an assessing gaze.

Cally felt her cheeks turn crimson.

'I thought so,' he drawled in amusement. 'But think just how good it will be when we do make love, *chérie.*'

'I might have been stupid enough to consider having sex with you before I knew who you were,' she said, trying not to flinch at the memory of her own wantonness. 'But I can assure you I am in no danger of doing so again.'

'You have a thing for university employees?' he queried, raising one long, lean finger to his lower lip thoughtfully, as if observing an anomalous result in a science experiment. 'Mediterranean princes just not your thing?'

No, men that self-important couldn't be any further from her thing, Cally thought, not that she had 'a thing'. So why in God's name was she unable to take her eyes off his mouth?

'Liars aren't my thing. Men who lie about who they are, who pretend not to be stinking rich and who profess to lend a sympathetic ear when—' Immediately the auction, which had slipped her mind for a moment, came back to her. The auction room. Leon the only one with the nonchalant glance. Not because he had nothing riding on it, but because he was so rich that he'd just instructed one of his minions to make the highest bid by phone on his behalf. That was why he had been there that night, to stand back and watch smugly whilst he blew everyone else out of the water. It had had nothing to do with coming back because he wanted her, and suddenly that hurt most of all. 'When all the time you were the one responsible for wrecking my career!'

Leon raised his eyebrows. 'Are you quite finished? Good. Firstly, I told you my name. You didn't ask what my surname was, nor did you give me yours. All I said was that I was in England in connection with my university. I was. The new University of Montéz has just been built at my say-so, and I was there to purchase some pieces for the art department. Since you chose where we should go, I can hardly be blamed if the bar you selected gave no indication of my wealth. Which brings me to your accusation that I offered to lend a sympathetic ear with regards to your career—on the contrary, it was you who insisted we should *not* discuss work. You simply chose to, I did not.'

'You consider being a prince a career choice?'

'Not a choice,' he said gravely. 'But my work, yes.'

'How convenient, rather like arguing that omitting the truth does not constitute a lie. If you and I were married—' Cally hesitated, belatedly aware that she couldn't have thought of a more preposterous example if she'd tried '—and you happened to be sleeping with another woman but just didn't mention it, would such an omission be tolerable?'

Leon's mouth hardened. Hadn't he just known that she was one of those women who had marriage on the brain?

'Tolerable? Marrying anyone would never be a tolerable scenario for me, Cally, so I'm afraid your analogy is lost.'

'What a surprise,' Cally muttered. 'When it proves that I'm absolutely right.' How utterly typical that he wasn't the marrying kind, she thought irritably, though she wasn't sure why she should care when she'd lost her belief in happy-ever-afters a long time ago.

'But surely a welcome surprise?' Leon seized the moment. 'For, rather than being the one responsible for wrecking your career, I think you'll find yourself eternally indebted to me for beginning it. What an accolade for your CV to be employed to restore two of the most famous paintings the world has ever known?'

Indebted to him; the thought horrified her. Yet he was also offering exactly what she had always wanted—well, almost. 'You said you were in London to purchase some pieces for the university's art department. Do you mean that once the Rénards are restored they will go on public display there?'

Leon lifted his arm sharply, the motion drawing back the sleeve of his shirt to reveal a striking Cartier watch. 'I would love to discuss the details now, but I'm afraid I have a meeting to attend with the principal of the university, as it happens. Much as I'm sure that, given your predilection for university staff, you'd find meeting Professor Lefevre *stimulating,* it is something I need to do alone. You and I can continue this discussion over breakfast.'

'I beg your pardon?'

'Breakfast. *Petit déjeuner.* The first meal of the day, *oui?*' He stared at her face, which was aghast. 'It is also a painting by Renoir, I believe—but, of course, you're the expert.'

Could he have any more of a cheek? 'I am well aware of the concept of breakfast, thank you. Just as I am well aware that I will be eating mine back in Cambridge tomorrow morning. You invited me here to discuss this *today.*'

'And I subsequently discovered that unfortunately today is the only day Professor Lefevre can have this meeting. But since you have nowhere else to be this can wait until tomorrow, *oui?*'

Cally seethed. 'I have a plane to catch. Home.'

'But how can you make the most important decision of your career without knowing all the facts?'

There was nothing to decide, was there? How could she even contemplate working for a man who had humiliated and lied to her? Because the job was everything she'd strived for, she thought ruefully. She recalled the hideous boss she'd once had at the gallery gift shop who'd paid her a pittance for running the place single-handedly, how she'd ignored him and had just knuckled down. She could do it again for her dream commission, couldn't she? But somehow she wasn't sure that ignoring Leon would be so easy. Unless she could do the restoration without his interference. Rent a studio by the seafront and work on the paintings there, only return here when she'd completed them. The idea seemed almost idyllic without the threat of his presence.

'If I stay for—for *breakfast,*' she repeated, the concept still ludicrous to her. 'You'll be open to discussion about how I would wish such a project to be completed?'

'Discussion? Of course.'

Cally did a mental calculation of whether she could afford one night in a French guesthouse, having presumed that she'd be back on a plane out of here this afternoon. She supposed that she *had* left that hotel in London a night earlier than planned…

'What time would you have me return?'

'I would have you here ready and waiting,' he said, beckoning for her to keep up with his brusque steps out of the ballroom and into the hallway, where the man who had driven her here was waiting compliantly, head bowed. 'This is Boyet. He will show you to your room and bring you dinner.'

And before she could argue the prince was gone.

CHAPTER FOUR

CALLY picked up her mobile phone from the bedside cabinet and stared at its neon display through the darkness. 2:48 a.m., and still awake. She had tried everything: lying on her back, on her front, and rather awkwardly on her side; shutting the window to block out the sound of the ocean in order to pretend that she was in her bed at home; opening the window in the hope that the ebb and flow of the sea would act as a natural lullaby. Finally she had tried to fool herself into sleep by pretending she didn't care whether she was awake or not. But still the minutes ticked by. And, the more the minutes ticked by, the more questions heaped up in her brain.

Why had she even come here? Life wasn't some fairy tale where princes were valiant men who did noble deeds. She, more than anyone, should know that a man who had been born into privilege was bound to be selfish and dishonest, and, if she'd forgotten, his arrogant email should have acted as a reminder. Perhaps it was because she'd been confident that he was *just* selfish and dishonest, and had thought she could deal with that. What she hadn't known was that the prince would also happen to be *him*. Yet how was that possible when she'd even tried to look him up? Especially as a couple of years ago, she hadn't been able to avoid photos of his late brother and his wife.

Cally took a deep breath and to her chagrin found herself wondering how Girard's death must have affected Leon, how terrible it must have been to lose a brother and to gain such responsibility in the same moment. But that presupposed he had a heart somewhere within his perfectly honed chest, she thought bitterly, and nothing about the way he had treated her suggested that he did. Had he chosen not to reveal who he was in London simply for his own amusement?

Probably. Just like he probably thought that a night in his opulent palace would make her feel like she owed him one. *As if.* The thought of being indebted to him in any way whatsoever made her feel sick. Which was why, despite feeling famished, she had rejected Boyet's offer of dinner last night. Which was why she had got into bed without using a single thing in the pale apricot bedroom, with its beautiful white furniture, including the array of luxurious toiletries laid out for her. Instead she had used the mishmash of bits and pieces she'd thrown in her handbag for freshening up on the flight—even if she hadn't been able to resist removing the lids of the eye-catching bottles and smelling each one in turn…

When Cally's alarm went off four hours later, she felt like an animal who had been disturbed from hibernation three months early. Thankfully with the morning came rational thought: that there was only one question that mattered, and that was whether or not he planned to offer her the job of working on her dream commission.

Which meant she had to treat this breakfast—however unwelcome the concept was to her—like a job interview.

A job interview she wished she could attend in something other than yesterday's crumpled suit, she thought uneasily as she walked towards the veranda where Boyet had told her she would find Leon at eight-twenty. At least she'd had the foresight to pack a change of underwear and a clean top.

Now that it was daylight, she noticed for the first time that this side of the palace had the most fantastic view of the bay below, the ocean so blue it reminded her of a glittering jewel. As she stepped onto the cream tiles of the patio, she was forced to admit that Leon gave the landscape a run for its money. He was sitting on a wrought-iron chair, one leg crossed over the other whilst he leafed through the day's *La Tribune,* looking more like a male model than a prince in his cool white linen shirt which had far less buttons done up than most other men could have got away with. On him, she thought shamefully, it seemed criminal not to be unbuttoned any more.

'You like the view?' he drawled, closing the paper.

Cally turned back to the horizon, all too aware that he had caught her out. 'I suppose it's on a par with the British coastline.' She shrugged, determined to remain indifferent to everything even remotely connected to him.

'Oh yes, this is England—just without rain,' he replied dryly as he motioned to the chair.

Cally sat, resting her portfolio on her knee, her back rigid and eyes lowered. The exact opposite of his languorous pose.

He ran his eyes openly over her face. 'You look terrible. Didn't you sleep?'

The insult cut her to the quick. She ought to be glad that he was through with faking desire where she was concerned, but it only made her feel worse. She could just imagine the kind of woman he was used to having breakfast with—perfectly made-up, top-to-toe designer. Just like Portia had been the morning she'd answered David's door sporting that enormous pink diamond.

'I'm afraid this is the way a woman who isn't plastered in make-up tends to look in the morning, Leon.'

He shook his head irritably. 'You are not the kind of woman who requires any make-up. I simply meant that you look a little—drained.'

The compliment caught her off guard, and she didn't know what to do with it. 'Actually, I could count the number of hours' sleep I've had on one hand. Without the use of my thumb.'

Leon stifled a smile and made a show of furrowing his brow as he poured her a strong black coffee without asking whether she wanted any. 'That suite has just been refurnished. I was assured that particular mattress was the best on the market. I will have to see that it is changed.'

How typical that he thought every problem in life could be solved by material goods, she thought irritably, trying to ignore the delicious scent of the coffee wafting invitingly up her nostrils. 'There was nothing wrong with the bed, save for the fact that it was under your roof.'

'Large houses have a few too many dark corners for you?' he suggested with feigned concern as Boyet appeared with a tray overflowing with food: spiced bread, honey, fruit with natural yogurt, freshly squeezed orange in two different jugs—one with pulp and one without. Cally's mouth watered, and she could feel her ravenous stomach start to rumble, but she cleared her throat to disguise it.

'Whilst you are right that it does have an unnecessarily large number of rooms, it had nothing to do with that. Believe it or not, I simply have no desire to be anywhere near you.'

'Yet you are still here.'

'Like you said, whatever my personal feelings, I would be foolish not to make this important decision in my career without discussing the facts.'

'Over breakfast.' He nodded as if her career was immaterial. 'But you are yet to have a sip of coffee or a morsel of any food. So, eat.'

It was tempting to say she wasn't hungry, but the tantalising aroma of nutmeg and sultanas was too enticing, and she succumbed to a piece of bread.

Leon watched her, thinking it was the most erotic thing he'd ever seen as she bit into it hungrily before twisting her rosebud of a mouth back into a look of disapproval.

'No woman I've ever invited to breakfast has ever tried so hard to look unhappy about it as you.'

Thinking about the different women who might have sat in this self-same seat before her for a second time made Cally fidget uncomfortably, and do up another button on her suit jacket despite the rising heat of the early-morning sunshine.

'Emotions are irrelevant, aren't they?' She slid her portfolio from her side of the table to his, telling herself to ignore his casual attire and the holiday setting and treat this in exactly the same way as she had treated her interview at the London City Gallery. 'This contains photographs of all my major restorations, as well as details of my qualifications. I specialised in Rénard for the theory side of my post-grad.'

He opened it casually, flicking to the first page and briefly reading through her CV as he sipped his coffee.

'You began studying for a fine-art degree in London,' he said thoughtfully, raising his head. 'But you didn't finish?'

Trust him to notice that first. She remembered the owner

of the London City Gallery getting to the same question at her second interview—remembered how, after all the years of hard work, she had finally felt able to answer it with confidence and integrity. So why did she feel so ashamed when *he* asked?

'No, I didn't complete it.' She drew in a deep breath. 'And it was a mistake not to. But for two years afterwards I worked a full-time job, and painted and studied in every spare moment I had. The Cambridge Institute then accepted me on their diploma in conservation based on my aptitude and commitment.'

'So why didn't you finish it?' Leon flicked her portfolio shut without looking at another page. 'Did you fall in love with a university professor and drop out in a fit of unrequited love?'

'I don't think that's relevant, do you?'

Leon saw a flash of something in her eyes which told him he had hit a raw nerve. He was tempted to probe deeper, but at the same time the thought of her having past lovers, let alone hearing about them, irritated him. Which was preposterous, because the women he slept with always matched him in experience.

He looked her straight in the eye. 'Actually, I happen to think the way someone behaves in personal relationships is indicative of the way they are likely to behave as an employee.'

Suddenly, the penny dropped in Cally's mind. So *that* was what London had been about. She felt herself grow even hotter beneath the fabric of her dark jacket as she realised what that meant. It had all been an underhand investigation into whether he considered her fit for the job, and she could only imagine what his conclusion had been!

Wasn't it just typical that the one night she had acted completely out of character was the one night that, unbeknown to her, she'd needed to be herself most of all? But what gave him the right to make such a judgement based on her behaviour, anyway? Just because he was a prince didn't give him permission to play at being some moral magistrate!

She challenged him right back with her gaze. 'Then you don't want to know what your behaviour indicates about you, *Your Highness.*'

'Since you are the one who wants to work on my paintings, my behaviour is irrelevant. Yours, on the other hand…'

'So why bother bringing me here if I've already failed your pathetic little personality test?'

His voice was slow and deliberate, 'Because, *chérie,* although you showed that your word cannot be trusted and that you are only interested in these paintings because you think they will bring you renown…' He paused, as if to revel in her horror. 'After extensive research into your abilities over the past week I happen to believe you are the best person for the job.'

Cally was so taken aback by the damning insult and high praise all delivered in one succinct sentence that she didn't know what to say—but before she had the chance to utter anything Leon continued. 'As a result, I wish to employ you. On one condition. There will be no *renown.* You may detail the commission in your portfolio, but that is it. On this island it is already forbidden for the press to print anything about me and my employees except in reference to the public work I carry out. It is a policy I do my best to ensure is reflected throughout the world, and which I expect all current and former staff to ensure is upheld. Indefinitely.'

Well, that explained the lack of information on the Web, Cally thought, perplexed that he seemed to think that that one condition might be her only bone of contention with his offer of employment, and at the same time wanting to ask if he'd ever heard of three little words known as 'freedom of press'.

She frowned. 'Yesterday you suggested that the Rénards were purchased for the university. Aren't they therefore part of your public work anyway?'

Leon raked a hand through his hair in irritation. Didn't he just know that she would try and twist it any way she could? 'No. The Rénards are for my private collection. I purchased a small Goya at the same auction for the university. Thankfully, it needs no restoration.'

Cally exploded. 'So the Rénards *are* to be treated like some trophy enjoyed by no one but you?'

He took a sip of coffee. 'If that is the way you choose to view my decision, *oui*. How fitting, then, that the two paintings themselves are a celebration of difference.'

Cally felt her temper flare, as much because his crude analysis matched her own studied interpretation of the paintings as at the discovery that he would be keeping them to himself.

'So you lied to me yet again.'

'I didn't lie, I just postponed the truth.' He shrugged nonchalantly. 'Are you going to pretend it makes a difference?'

'Of course it does!'

'Really? As I recall it, you told me that despite your oh-so-ethical principles nothing would stop you working on the paintings. Unless…'

'Unless what?'

'Unless you are going to go back on your word. Again.'

His eyes met hers in smouldering challenge. He was baiting her, she knew he was, and every instinct within her screamed *walk away*. He *had* bought the paintings for no other reason than as an acquisition to boast about. He *was* a damned liar. And she had never felt so humiliated by any other man in her life. *Or so alive.*

But just what would she be walking away to—a blank diary and a pile of bills? Only now it would be worse, because she would know that she had walked away from her dream restoration for the sake of what boiled down to her pride. And, worse, though she hated to admit she gave a damn about what he thought, he would believe that she *was* incapable of sticking to her word, of seeing things through. The very trait that, after that one mistake, she'd spent years proving was not part of her character.

If she turned him down, the only person who would lose out was her. Leon would simply employ someone else to do the work, and a man with more money than morals would have thwarted her dreams for the second time in her life. The thought set free a deep-rooted ball of fury inside her. So what if he and his plans for the paintings were the antithesis of everything she believed in? For once in her life, why the hell shouldn't she turn that to her advantage?

'Do you wish me to begin work straight away?'

'That depends. Will you sign a contract which states that your employment will terminate if you break the condition?'

'I see no reason why not.'

'Then this afternoon suits me.'

Cally smiled a sickly smile, determined to make this difficult. 'In which case, I will require some payment up front in order to rent somewhere to stay, and—'

'Somewhere to *rent?*' he said with unconcealed disgust.

She nodded.

'And why on earth would that be necessary when, as you have already pointed out, the palace has an excess of rooms?'

'Because…because I hardly think living as well as working here is appropriate, under the circumstances.'

His raised his eyebrow. 'Circumstances?'

She felt a whole new level of heat wash over her and wished she had never opened her mouth. 'You know what I mean.'

'If we had slept together I would see your point, *ma belle,* but since you were so vehement that we should not there is no problem, *d'accord?*'

Yes, there is a bloody great problem, Cally thought, *and its despicably handsome face is staring right at me.*

'Fine. So I shall stay here and work here. But I'll need my conservation equipment.' She looked down at her suit and back up at him. 'And, as I thought I was only going to be here for a matter of hours, I'll need my clothes sent from home as well. Surely you can't deny that I shall be needing those for the duration of my stay?' she spat out, before she had time to realise that such a statement was just asking to be twisted.

'Only time will tell, Cally,' he purred. The way the two syllables of her name dropped from his tongue reminded her of hot, liquid chocolate, and she felt a bead of sweat trickle down between her breasts. 'But there will be no need to send for anything,' he drawled, as if her suggestion was utterly ridiculous. 'I will have everything you could possibly need brought over from Paris, a new wardrobe included.'

'I don't need a new wardrobe!'

He ran his eyes over her suit critically. 'Oh, but I think you do.'

Cally's cheeks burned at his insult, her body temperature continuing to rocket. 'Well, then, it's lucky I don't care what you think, isn't it?'

'Lucky? I'd say irrelevant is more accurate,' he said, draining his cup of coffee.

'But…!' Cally glared at him, her whole body teeming with frustration, but he simply ignored her and carried on.

'In the meantime, I presume you will wish to examine the *paintings.*' He emphasised it insultingly, as if she was the one getting sidetracked. 'Make a list of all the materials you will require and pass it on to Boyet by the end of the day. He will see that they are ordered immediately.' He ran his eyes over her figure as he stood up. 'And although it will be tomorrow before the clothes arrive from Paris I'm sure it wouldn't kill you to remove that jacket sometime before then. You look like you're about to pass out.'

Leon got to his feet and Cally stumbled to do the same, determined that this meeting would not end up with him walking away from her. 'You may be used to women fainting in your presence, Leon, but I can assure you that you leave me completely cold.'

'Well, if this is cold, *chérie,* I can't wait to see you fired up,' he mocked, and before she could even attempt to beat him away from the table he was halfway back to the palace, so that to her consternation it simply looked as though she had been standing ceremoniously for his exit.

'Then I hope you're a very patient man,' she yelled back, and, seeing that he had already entered the glass doors, allowed herself to drop back into her chair and tear off the blasted jacket.

'I'm not sure patience will be necessary,' he drawled as he pulled back the inside blind and dropped his eyes to her blouse. 'Are you?'

CHAPTER FIVE

'WOULD you have me carry these to your room now, Mademoiselle Greenway?'

Cally gawped in disbelief as she descended the stairs the following morning to find Boyet surrounded by countless bags and boxes. It reminded her of the sea of gifts that had spilled out from beneath the ten-foot pine at David's house that Christmas eight years ago, and his subsequent withering expression when she'd taken him back to meet her parents and he'd seen their sparse equivalent. It immediately soured her mood.

'I suppose there must be something suitable for work hidden in one of them, Boyet, thank you. Here, let me give you a hand.'

Despite his protests, Cally helped Boyet carry the fifty-four bags and boxes upstairs, but after peeling back enough tissue paper to completely bury the bedroom carpet she discovered that her supposition had been wrong. Yes, in amongst the high-heeled shoes, cocktail dresses and a disturbing amount of lingerie there was the odd pair of fine linen trousers and a single pair of diamanté designer jeans, but there was nothing she would have considered even remotely suitable for getting covered in paint. In fact it was the kind of wardrobe that would better befit a mistress than a woman he'd employed to do a job that could be both mentally and physically exhausting.

Maybe that was because it *was* a mistress's wardrobe, Cally thought cynically as she recalled Leon's comment yesterday which had implied just how frequently women joined him for breakfast. He probably had the whole lot on standby and simply ordered a new batch whenever he chose someone new to warm his bed. Well, she thought bitterly, her purpose here was not to dress for his pleasure. Not that she supposed for one minute that she was in any danger of that; whatever attraction he'd feigned towards her in London had simply been an elaborate plan to test her suitability for this job, hadn't it? She didn't know why that got to her most of all, when the real reason why she was angry was that he obviously had no concept of a woman needing clothes to work in. Well, she thought, grabbing for the designer jeans and rooting around in her handbag, she would soon see to that.

Cally doubted that her nail scissors would ever be fit for their intended purpose again, but twenty minutes later she felt rebelliously gleeful as she redescended the stairs and headed to the studio wearing the freshly cut-off, diamanté-less jeans, which now ended mid-thigh, and a royal blue silk blouse knotted at her waist.

The studio was triple the size of the room she used for restorations back home in Cambridge, but compared to everything she had encountered in the palace so far it was surprisingly understated. Aside from the tall glass doors which faced the sea and let in an ideal abundance of natural light, the room contained very little save for a row of cupboards, a sink, a comfy-looking sofa covered with a red throw and a CD player in the corner.

And of course the Rénards, which now dominated the space. She had been sitting alone on the veranda after breakfast yesterday, her jacket still tossed aside in frustration, when Boyet had approached to inform her that the paintings were being set up on easels in here for her to begin her assessment. Relieved to be able to concentrate on practicalities, her mood had instantly turned to one of resolve. When she had taken Boyet the list of materials she anticipated she would need for the duration of the restoration later that afternoon, she had been even more relieved to hear that Leon had gone out on royal business and would not be back until after dark.

However, though Leon seemed to be leaving her to it this morning as well, Cally was perplexed to find that she was not consumed by the single-mindedness she usually felt when confronted with a new commission, and which she had expected to have in spades when it came to the Rénards.

She pulled up her stool before the masterpieces and drew in a deep breath, forcing herself to block out everything else, but her mind was still running riot. Perhaps it was too quiet. She was used to the buzz of traffic outside her window back home. She went over to the CD player and ran her fingers along the shelf of jewelled cases, surprised to find there was more than one rock album amongst his collection. She hesitated over one of them. Tempting though it was to put it on, she knew it would only serve to remind her of *that* night, and that was bound to skew her thoughts completely. So she put on some contemporary jazz, told herself a prince didn't buy his own CDs anyway, and sat down again.

Being able to focus was her speciality; it always had been. She cast her mind back to her conservation course in Cambridge. There had been plenty of students with more natural talent than she had, but, to quote the words of her tutor, no one who applied themselves in quite the same way that she did. Whilst other students had partied till dawn, and only started thinking about their assignments on the day of a deadline, Cally would be finished with weeks to spare, already working on the next. Maybe it was because she had fought so hard for a second chance. Or maybe it was because since that moment in Mrs McLellan's class all those years before her passion for art had surpassed everything.

Even though her epiphany had initially taken the form of wanting to be an artist in the traditional sense, Cally admitted, unsure why that thought was accompanied by a deep pang of regret today when usually she could view her change of vocation objectively. It was probably because, if she had been able to bring herself to paint any of her paltry compositions after her split with David, even they would have had more chance of appearing in a public gallery than the two most impressive nineteenth-century paintings in existence. Cally balled her hands into fists. How was it possible that a man who was opening a university which encouraged learning about art could keep these incredible paintings for his eyes only? The university was just a princely duty, she supposed, a role which was separate from his own sentiments. Which was exactly how she needed to view this job.

'Before shots, that's where I should start,' Cally said aloud, as if talking to herself might drown out her tumultuous thoughts and help with her focus. She reached into her bag and found her battered camera, then took a step backwards, lining up the lens.

'Thinking of your precious portfolio, *chérie?*'

At the sound of his voice she dropped her hand guiltily. As soon as she did, she realised how ridiculous that was, but by then her hand was too unsteady to continue.

Only because he had made her jump, Cally reasoned. How had he snuck in without her hearing? She was annoyed that she had no way of knowing how long he'd been standing there watching her, and made a mental note to lower the volume on the CD player in future, though the music was far from loud.

'Having a record of their initial appearance for reference is an essential part of the process,' she said defensively, turning to face him. The sight caught her off guard. He was perched on the arm of the sofa in a pair of faded light blue jeans that moulded his thighs, and a white T-shirt that revealed the taut plane of his stomach, the casual attire doing nothing to belittle the power he seemed to exude naturally. She swallowed slowly, her mouth suddenly feeling parched. 'Was there something you wanted?'

'I just came to check you hadn't been attacked by the palace lawnmower,' he drawled, producing two pieces of hacked-off denim. 'Stéphanie was a little concerned to find these whilst cleaning your room.'

Cally's mouth twitched into a smile. 'Well, as you can see, I'm absolutely fine.'

'It's a shame I can't say the same for the jeans.'

'What's a shame is that you didn't allow me to have my own clothes sent from home. How am I supposed to do my job wearing some skintight, dry-clean-only designer outfit?

You're lucky I didn't decide to do a Julie Andrews and take to your curtains instead.'

'Sorry?' Her words shook Leon out of his state of semi-arousal. Ever since he'd entered the room he'd been transfixed by her pert little bottom and her long, shapely legs in her makeshift shorts. Until she'd just revealed that her outing with the scissors had all been a protest because he hadn't let her have her own way.

'You know—Julie Andrews in *The Sound of Music*— where she makes clothes for all the children out of the curtains. Didn't you ever see it?'

'I can't say that I did.'

Cally looked at him with new eyes, truly comprehending for the first time that he wasn't just Mr Drop-dead Gorgeous with whom she'd shared one earth-shattering kiss before he'd humiliated and lied to her. He was royalty, the sole ruler of a Mediterranean island. Whilst she'd spent the school holidays watching old movies with her sister whilst her parents were out at work, what must he have been doing—opening the odd university here, making a state visit there?

Yet, even though he owned this luxurious palace, had the title and the sense of self-importance to match, she still found it somehow difficult to imagine. Maybe it was because he'd described his role here as if it was just a job. But that was ridiculous, because being royal wasn't an occupation, it was who he was. So how was it that he had seemed to fit right into that bar in London when he ought to have stuck out like a Van Gogh in a public toilet?

Cally quickly returned her camera to her bag and moved back to her seat, appalled to realise that she had been inadvertently giving him the once-over. 'Don't you have royal duties this morning?'

Leon had never been so glad that someone had elected to sit on a stool rather than a chair as he watched the waistband of her shorts come tantalisingly close to revealing the top of the perfect globes of her bottom. 'Not until my meeting later with the president of France.'

'Oh.' It took all Cally's powers of concentration to transfer a bottle of distilled water into a small beaker without pouring it all over her lap. 'Then I'm sure you must have a lot to prepare.'

'If it's not distracting, I thought I might watch you quietly.'

It wasn't really even a question, and if it was then he had asked it so airily it was impossible to answer that, actually, she felt seriously in danger of putting the cotton bud through the canvas if he stayed. She'd worked in front of people heaps of times before—students, enthusiastic clients—and, for goodness' sake, the first step of the process was only removing the dirt and grime. All it required was a little focus.

'As you wish.'

Leon witnessed her hesitation and smiled to himself. 'You can begin without the supplies from Paris?'

Cally felt herself marginally relax, glad to talk about work. 'The cleaning, yes. It's more a case of time and patience than apparatus in the early stages.'

'Like so many things,' he said, deliberately slowly.

She told herself she was imagining his suggestive tone. 'I had a tutor who used to say that half the work is in the diagnosis. Each painting is like a patient. The symptoms might be similar, but working out the treatment is unique to every one.'

An image of Cally wearing a nurse's uniform and tending to him in bed popped into Leon's head, and the erection which had begun at the sight of her legs in those shorts grew even harder.

'So, did you always want to restore art?'

As Cally returned to her seat she felt the muscles in her shoulders go taut. 'I started out wanting to be an artist in the traditional sense, but things changed. I don't do my own work anymore.'

She waited for the snide comment, the probing questions, but was surprised to find they didn't come.

'Our lives don't always follow the course we expect, *non?*'

'No,' she said, somehow finding the courage to begin in the top corner of the first painting. 'They don't.'

He must be referring to his brother's death, Cally thought, for it occurred to her that, if Girard had lived, then Leon might never have become prince. She wanted to ask him about it, but at the same time felt bound to show him the same quiet respect.

He broke the momentary silence. 'But providence works in mysterious ways, wouldn't you say?'

'I'd say that view of the world is a little romantic for me.'

She heard him move and saw on the periphery of her vision that he was leaning up against the cupboards to her left, contemplating her profile.

'You mean you do not believe in romance, *ma belle?*'

She dipped the cotton bud back in the distilled water and deflected the question. 'Why, do you?'

'I am a Frenchman, Cally.' He laughed a low, throaty laugh. 'It's in my blood.'

'How curious, when only yesterday you were telling me that you find the idea of marriage intolerable.'

He eyed her sceptically. 'What amazing powers of recollection you have for someone who professed to have no interest in the subject.'

'A good memory is essential for my job,' she replied a little too quickly. 'In order to recall the mixes of different chemicals.'

'Of course.' He stroked a hand across his chin with mock sincerity. 'Your job. That is what we were discussing, after all. So, tell me, is it coincidence that you chose to start with the fully clothed portrait before moving on to the nude, or is the significance intentional?'

Cally's hand was poised in mid-air an inch away from the canvas. 'I'm sorry?'

'Is it deliberate that you have begun on the work which has the least damage first?'

She pursed her lips, knowing that he hadn't been implying anything so innocuous.

'Yes. It allows me to get accustomed to the necessary techniques before moving on to the larger areas of damage.'

'The patient requiring the most intensive treatment.' He nodded seriously, startling her with the evidence that he had been listening thoroughly to her earlier explanation.

He saw her falter a second time and stifled a grin. 'I am sorry. I promised to watch quietly. I will leave you to carry on in peace, if you'll just excuse me whilst I just pick up a couple of things?'

Cally inclined her head, thinking how impeccable his manners could be when he wanted. She did not really take in what he was saying until she saw him move to the cupboard at the front of the room and remove a towel.

'I thought they were all empty, ready for the paint supplies,' she commented.

'They are, except for these few. I've got rid of the majority of my equipment now I have so few chances to use it.'

'Equipment?'

'Diving equipment,' he explained, before catching sight of the intense curiosity on her face which told him that it had not been clarification enough. He supposed no harm could come from telling her. 'Before it became necessary for me to rule the island, I worked as a diver for the Marine Nationale.'

Cally tried to hide the astonishment she felt. 'The French Navy?' As an admiral or a captain she could well imagine, but a diver? She swallowed as he hooked his thumbs under the corner of his T-shirt. It certainly explained his incredible physique—in which she had absolutely no interest, of course. It was just that she'd been trained to admire things that were aesthetically pleasing.

'This room is closest to the sea. I used to train out of here before I signed up full-time.'

Cally watched, her whole body besieged by a frightening and unfamiliar paralysis as he revealed his taut, muscular chest and exceptionally broad shoulders. He had a scar, she noticed, running from just below his belly button to somewhere below the waistband of his jeans. The mark of his fallibility fascinated her. How had he got it? How would it feel to trace its pale crease with her fingertips and find out where it led—and, more to the point, why was she even wondering? Her pulse skittered madly. Good God, now he was unbuttoning his flies! She moved her face closer to the painting, pretending to look at it closely, willing herself to concentrate on Rénard's artistic genius. But the live work of nature before her was suddenly a whole lot more impressive.

When she raised her head to look again he was wearing pale blue swimming trunks, and she found herself inexplicably frustrated that she had no way of knowing whether he had been wearing them underneath his jeans all along or not.

'We haven't had a day this hot for weeks.' His mouth twitched in amusement as he walked over to the small fridge by the sink and took a long swig from a bottle of water. *Try years,* Cally thought, her mouth growing dry at the sight. They ought to use him to advertise mineral water. Or on second thoughts perhaps not; it would probably cause a drought.

'It's definitely even warmer than yesterday,' she replied weakly.

'So join me.' He nodded at the inviting blue glitter of sea outside the window.

Join him? She followed his gaze and imagined plunging into its cooling depths. Then she turned her attention back to the tanned, muscular profile. Far, far too dangerous.

'Thanks, but it could be detrimental not to complete this part of the process now I've started.'

'Of course,' he said slowly. 'Just don't get too hot in here all by yourself.'

And with that he opened the glass doors, strolled the short distance to the cliff and dived in.

Several minutes passed before Cally realised she was still staring at the empty space where he had been, her cotton bud poised inanely in mid-air. Racked with irritation that the ability to apply herself to her work was now even further from her grasp, she dropped the bud back into the container of water and stood up, hoping that stretching her legs and turning off the CD player would allow her to regroup her thoughts. But before she could stop herself she was stretching her legs back across the room to the wide glass doors.

Cally touched a hand to her hair and looked behind her guiltily as she got closer to the threshold between inside and out. Which was ridiculous, because she was perfectly entitled to get up and look at the view, and it wasn't as though anyone could see her anyway. She peered over the cliff edge and down into the expanse of blue below, then across the bay, out at the horizon and back again. It was so still there was hardly a wave. So where was he? She tried to pretend she didn't care, that she was taking in the amazingly cloudless sky as her eyes frantically skimmed the water. Until—thank goodness—there he was, returning to the surface.

However much she wanted to argue to some invisible jury that she was just admiring the glorious landscape, the sight of him held her transfixed. His muscular shoulders were stretched tight, his strong arms slicing rhythmically through the water; he was so focussed that she was not only mesmerised but envious. He dipped beneath the surface, sometimes for so long that she almost did herself an injury as she strained to see below the water, each reappearance causing a clammy wash of relief across her shoulders and down her back.

Shockingly, half of her—like the woman in the paintings—felt the unprecedented impulse to brazenly remove her clothes and follow him into the sea. Her more sensible half told her that that was not only inexcusable, because she was his employee, but that she had to be deranged if she thought she had anything in common with the siren in Rénard's painting. So why as she watched him was she unable to stop herself running her hands over the silk of her blouse as if to check it hadn't disappeared of its own accord? And why did she feel the urge to close her eyes and explore the unfamiliar ache pooling between her thighs as her hand lingered over her breasts?

Because you're a fool, Cally, a voice inside her screamed at the exact moment that the memory of his kiss on the dark and crowded dance floor flew into her mind, and she suddenly remembered the auction. Remembered that he had lied to her from the moment she had met him, and that even if he hadn't, thinking about him that way could only lead to disappointment. So why was she standing here allowing herself to feel this way—no matter that they were feelings she could never recall ever feeling before—when she was supposed to be working on her dream commission?

It was because the thrill of getting this job had been diminished by the way in which it had come about, she thought pragmatically, knotting her hands behind her and walking back towards the paintings. It was discovering that her employer was not only the epitome of everything she loathed, but that he was also the man who had dented her pride on the first occasion in years when she had actually dared to live a little. If the London City Gallery had won the paintings the night of the auction, everything would have been different; she would have rung her family, euphoria would have hit and single-minded focus would have followed. Yes, Cally thought, what she needed was to be reminded of the enormity of this opportunity, to talk to someone who would know how much it meant to her.

She bent down and rifled through her handbag in search of her paint-smattered mobile, scrolling through the short-list of contacts until she found her sister's number.

Jen answered amidst the usual sea of background noise

which seemed to follow her around; if it wasn't the sound of Dylan and Josh using each other as climbing frames, then it was the hustle and bustle of a breaking news story. This time it sounded like the latter.

'Cally? Are you OK?'

'Hi, Jen, I'm fine,' Cally replied, unsure why her sister's voice was loaded with concern. Although she'd wanted to talk about it, she hadn't told Jen anything about Montéz. Last time they'd spoken she'd been ninety percent sure that the email was a hoax, and, when the tickets had arrived, she'd decided it would be prudent to wait and see if it actually yielded a job first, rather than have to report back with another story of rejection if it didn't. 'Is it a bad time to talk?'

'No, not at all—I'm outside Number Ten waiting for the prime minister to emerge, but I could be here for hours. It's just that I left a message on your answer phone inviting you to dinner on Sunday and you haven't replied.'

'When was that?'

'Last night.'

Last night? She hadn't replied in less than twenty-four hours and that automatically made her sister think something was up? Cally pulled at a loose thread on her shorts and frowned. She'd always thought her swiftness to reply to people was a positive thing—she was the first one to send out thank-yous after Christmas, always RSVP-ing on time to invitations to weddings and parties, even if it was to decline them. Only now did she realise how much it screamed 'I need to get out more'.

'Thanks, but I'm afraid I can't come. I'm in Montéz.'

'Montéz?' The utter disbelief in her sister's voice bugged her. 'Good for you. It's about time you had a holiday.'

'I'm not on holiday. I'm working on the Rénards.'

'Cally, that's fantastic! How? Tell me everything. You found out who bought them?'

'The buyer found me.'

'That's because you're the best person for the job. Didn't I tell you that was a possibility? So, who is it?'

Cally hesitated, not having foreseen that this discussion would inevitably end up being about the very person she was trying to put out of her mind. 'He's the prince here.'

There was a shocked pause. 'Oh my God—don't tell me you're working for Leon Montallier?'

Cally almost dropped the phone. 'How on earth do *you* know his name?'

Jen whistled through her teeth. 'Everyone who works for a paper knows his name. We're just not allowed to print anything about him. Not that anybody knows anything—he's too much of an enigma.'

'Too much of a bastard,' Cally corrected, turning to pace in the other direction as she realised that during the conversation she'd walked herself dangerously close to the glass doors once more. 'There's nothing else worth knowing.'

'Hang on a minute. Hasn't he just given you your dream job?'

'Yes, he has,' Cally admitted, trying to sound enthused as she recalled that this was the whole purpose for her call. 'And the chance to infill for a master like Rénard is incredible but—'

'But what? Oh, don't tell me that because he's royalty he thought that gave him the right to try it on?'

The frankness Jen had developed from her years reporting on the wealthy and powerful usually amused Cally, but today its accuracy—or rather its inaccuracy—only succeeded in making her feel more wretched.

'But he doesn't plan to display the pictures in a gallery, that's what. They're nothing more than a symbol of his nauseating wealth.'

'Well, I can't say I'm surprised about that, I'm afraid,' Jen said, unaware how close her initial remark had been to the bone. 'But that doesn't mean you can't share your restoration process with the public, does it?'

'Sorry?'

'The paper could run a story. Our arts specialist, Julian, would kill to do a piece on it!'

'I *wish*. But he's so anti-press that it's written into my contract that I can't even— Jen?'

The volume of the background noise suddenly doubled, and Cally could hear the clash of a thousand cameras and the sound of bodies jostling forward.

'Jen, can you hear me?'

'Sorry, sis, gotta go!'

''Course—look, just forget I even mentioned him, OK?'

Leon's mouth curved in amusement as he approached the studio doors to find her concentrating hard on facing the wall as she finished her call. She was making a show of trying to stick to her word, he'd give her that. But, if it was for his benefit, she needn't bother. Didn't she know that he had seen her from the water? And didn't she know that it made no difference whether he witnessed it or not?

Her desire for him was written into every move her delectable body made. It had been from the very first moment she had looked at him with those expressive green eyes. He wondered how much longer she would keep fighting it, pretending that what mattered to her were the paintings. Had she forgotten how clear she had made it in that insalubrious bar in London? Had she forgotten that she had told him she was only interested in this job to gain renown? Since he had made sure *that* wasn't an option, her reason for accepting was obvious—him. But, then, he was well aware that women were experts at pretending to be driven by their careers in order to entice a man. Women who claimed to have moved on from their nineteenth-century counterparts, who learned a handful of accomplishments to try and coerce a man into marrying them, but who really hadn't changed at all. They had simply got more devious.

Not that Cally was claiming to want *marriage,* he thought dryly. But he didn't doubt that those wistful looks into jewellers' windows would inevitably come if he kept her in his bed for too long.

'Someone special?'

Cally jumped and swung round to see him crossing the studio as the deep timbre of his voice reverberated through her body. How the hell hadn't she heard him come in this time? She looked down, convinced he mustn't be wearing shoes. She was right, but for her gaze to have alighted on the bareness of his toes was a mistake. Not only did she notice that even his feet were impossibly sexy, but it only encouraged her to sweep her eyes upwards over the damp hairs clinging to his legs, to the towel slung about his waist and his mouth-watering chest.

'Sorry?'

'The phone call. It must have been someone special, to interrupt what you were doing when you seemed so reluctant to stop.'

'I—I'd finished the section I was on. I'm just about to start on the next.' She sat back down in the chair and made to pick up a fresh cotton bud.

He looked at her with amusement dancing in his eyes. 'I wasn't talking about the paintings.'

Cally froze and felt herself blush redder than her hair as she realised what he meant. Wanting to die of embarrassment, she clutched around in her mind for some feasible excuse as to why she had been looking out to sea with her hands on her body, but it didn't come.

He broke into a wry smile and continued. 'But, much as I would like to watch you continue, I'm afraid I cannot keep the French president waiting.' Cally swallowed as he removed the towel from around his waist and laid it around his shoulders. 'I will be back tomorrow evening, when the Sheikh of Qwasir and his new fiancée will be coming for dinner. I thought perhaps you might like to join us, show them what you're working on.'

Cally stared at him, her embarrassment turning to astonishment. Firstly that he had even asked her, and secondly that, despite his own rebuttal of the press, he socialised with two people who could not have had a higher media profile.

'You mean the couple who are on the front of every newspaper in the world?'

Leon tensed and gave a single nod.

'And you wish me to show them the paintings?' Even though she hated the idea of private buyers wanting famous artwork for no other reason than to impress their friends, she couldn't help feeling both excited and honoured at the prospect of getting to share them with anyone.

'That is what I said,' Leon ground out, only now aware that, whilst he had envisioned a night with her beside him wearing one of those figure-hugging dresses he had selected, she saw it only as an opportunity to get herself known amongst the rich and famous.

'Thank you—then I'm delighted to accept.'

'Of course you are,' he drawled, before walking over to the table and handing her the cotton bud she was still yet to pick up. 'In the meantime, I'm sure you'll want to get on with what you came here to do.'

CHAPTER SIX

GET ON with what you came here to do. Leon's sarcastic words were still reverberating through Cally's mind as she tramped upstairs twenty-four hours later. If only she could. More than anything that was what she wanted, but to her horror another day had passed unproductively. Even though the supplies she needed had arrived that morning, even though she'd had the palace to herself, she hadn't been able to stop herself from gazing up at the glass doors, imagining him rising half-naked from the sea.

Allowing herself to get distracted in any way at all was completely unlike her, she thought as she entered the bedroom, never mind by thoughts of that nature. Everything she ever took on she always committed to one hundred and ten per cent until it was complete. Except her fine-art degree, she admitted ruefully. Was that it then— every time she met a man she found remotely attractive she was reduced to a mess of distraction which robbed her of all her artistic focus?

Cally cast her mind back to the summer she had met David, when she had taken a job as a waitress at the tearoom in the grounds of his father's stately home. Had she been so bowled over by his charms that it had rendered her completely incapable of holding a brush? No, she thought frankly, actually, she hadn't. She'd been flattered by the unexpected attention he'd bestowed upon her, naively impressed by the upper-class world in which he lived, but she certainly hadn't felt this kind of paralysis. That was not what had made her throw in her studies, it was that she'd foolishly believed him when he'd said she would never become a great artist spending all her time working towards a degree. Only later had she discovered that, just like his chauvinistic father, the idea of a woman going to university had appalled him, particularly one whose father was just a postman.

So why the hell was it this way with Leon? Cally wondered as she opened her wardrobe to find it had been miraculously filled with the contents of the fifty-four bags and boxes whilst she had been working—and to her amusement some additional T-shirts and casual cut-offs too. And why was she so tempted to wear one of the glamorous dresses now, when she loathed the excess they represented? Because his guests were an esteemed desert ruler and a model, which meant such an outfit was appropriate for this element of her work in the same way her sister's black dress had been necessary for the auction, Cally justified, feeling both apprehensive and thrilled at the prospect of talking about the paintings. Even if talking about them was all she was able to do at the moment.

In the end she selected a beautiful jade dress with an asymmetric hem that felt so good swishing around her legs as she came down the stairs that, when she reached the grand dining room, it took her a minute to process that the table was completely bare. She looked at the antique clock on the wall, wondering if she had got the time wrong. Noting she hadn't, she decided she must have been mistaken about the place. Heaven knew, the palace was big enough, and Leon could hold the soirée in any number of rooms.

'Boyet!' Cally caught sight of him just as he was about to turn the corner of the inner stairs. 'I was supposed to meet His Highness in the dining room for the royal dinner at eight. Is it to be held elsewhere?'

'I believe there has been a change of plan altogether, mademoiselle.' He looked at the floor, evidently embarrassed that he was in possession of information that she was not. 'The last time I saw His Royal Highness, he was headed outside, as if he intended to go diving.'

'In *this*?' Cally gasped, concern furrowing her brow as she looked out across the hallway and through the high windows towards the inky blue sky, the rising wind beginning to whip against the glass.

'Thank you, Boyet,' she replied with a quick but earnest nod, turning on her three-inch heels in matching jade and hastening to the studio with none of the ladylike elegance with which she had just descended the stairs.

The room was bathed in darkness, and her pace slowed as she approached the glass doors; she was almost afraid of coming upon the view of the sea too quickly for fear of what she might see. Eventually she reached the handle and, finding it locked, began fumbling around in search of a key.

'Looking for something?'

Cally turned sharply to find Leon sitting absolutely still on the sofa, bathed in shadows. The look of accusation in his eyes matched the warning tone of his voice.

'Boyet said you were out in this.' She raised one hand out towards the blackness of the ocean, as if the concept was the most preposterous thing she had ever heard, choosing to overlook his equally sinister mood. As far as she could see, she was the only one who had a reason to be angry.

'I was,' he said abruptly as she turned on the lamp next to the paintings, softly illuminating the room.

He was dressed in jeans and a T-shirt that clung to his body in such a way that she could see his skin beneath was still damp. His hair was dark and heavy with moisture. If she hadn't been so determined not to think it, she would have admitted it was the most alluring thing she had ever seen in her life.

'Are you insane?'

'Insane to risk being late for our high-profile dinner engagement?' he drawled, eyeing her so critically that all the joy she'd felt in wearing the jade dress evaporated.

'To go diving tonight, when the ocean is so restless,' Cally corrected, wondering how he wasn't shivering with cold when just thinking about being in the water had her arms breaking out in goose bumps. 'Isn't one scar enough?'

Leon's mouth twitched into a sardonic smile. 'Though your observational skills are as touching as your concern, I can assure you that swimming in the cove outside my back door is hardly a risk in comparison to defusing a mine one hundred metres below sea level. I'll admit it's been a while, but—'

'Fine.' Cally blushed furiously. 'So, what about dinner? Boyet said there had been a change of plan.'

'There has. Unfortunately Kaliq and Tamara are unable to join us. Exhaustion after their journey here, I believe.'

'And you didn't think it polite to tell me before I went to the trouble of getting dressed up?'

'Given your track record, I had no idea you would go to so much trouble.' He stared at her legs, remembering where her shorts had been. 'But, then, I suppose I should have known, shouldn't I?'

'Known what?' Cally swiped, growing increasingly frustrated at his unaccountably bad mood.

'That everything's different when you're presented with the chance of renown.'

'Renown?' She turned to him blankly.

'God, you really are good, aren't you?' His mouth twisted in disgust.

'Good at what, Leon? At least tell me what the hell I've done so I can *try* and defend myself.'

He had flung it before she'd even finished speaking. It narrowly missed the first painting, hitting the lamp, which crashed to the floor, by luck avoiding the easel of the second painting by less than an inch. It was only after she'd thrown herself in front of both Rénards as if to shield them from further attack that she realised that it was a rolled-up newspaper.

'What the hell do you think you're playing at?'

'I was about to ask you the same question.'

'What?' she cried in exasperation. 'You're the one who just nearly destroyed an eighty-million-pound work of art!'

'*My* eighty-million-pound work of art,' he replied smoothly. 'Which I was nowhere near. It's a shame I can't say the same for you and the press.'

Grasping that there was something she was missing, Cally was already on the floor, unrolling the paper, cringing as she saw the teaser at the top of the page.

THE WORLD TODAY

Restoring our interest: Rénard's masterpieces since *that* auction.

Art conservator Cally Greenway shares her eighty-million-pound secret!

Cally's eyes widened in horror. She'd told her sister that running an article was out of the question, hadn't she? Cally's cheeks coloured as she fought to remember the details, details which were hazy because at the time she'd been so distracted by the thought of *him*. Yes, she most definitely had, and she knew there was no way that Jen would run a story regardless. Unless…unless in all the commotion on the other end of the line her sister hadn't heard her properly.

'There's been a mistake,' Cally cried helplessly. 'I told her not to print anything.'

'Her?'

'My sister Jen's a journalist.'

'Oh, fantastic.'

Cally's voice became defensive. 'I only called her because I wanted to share the fact that I'd got the job I thought I'd lost.' His expression was utterly remorseless. 'In the same way *she* calls *me* about what's going on in her life. She happened to mention that an article about restoring the Rénards would be a great way of sharing them with the public. I agreed that it *would* be, but I told her there was no way you'd allow it. But…but we got cut off, and she must have misunderstood what I'd said.'

'How convenient for you.'

'Are you calling me a liar?'

Leon looked at her patronisingly. 'I'm saying that, if you think I have forgotten that night in London, then you are even more foolish than I thought.'

Cally coloured instantly. 'What has this got to do with London?'

'You mean you have forgotten, *chérie?*' he drawled, his eyes lingering on her lips. 'You told me your reason for wanting to work on the Rénards. It was so that your name would be known across the world, was it not? So how can you possibly expect me to believe that this exposure is an accident?'

'I told you! Jen must have misunderstood. Let me call her, get to the bottom of it—'

'I think calling her once has done enough damage, don't you?'

Cally let out a frustrated sigh. 'And for that I'm sorry, but…' She scanned her eyes down the article, and noticed that the 'secret' the headline referred to was nothing more than the fact that she was restoring the paintings for a private collector in France. 'Look.' She pointed to the text. 'You're not even mentioned. Yes, that the article exists is a mistake. But everyone makes mistakes now and again—' she hesitated '—even you.'

'But this isn't about me.' He paused, and then the tone of his voice suddenly turned. 'Unless, of course, what you are really trying to tell me is that I'm *precisely* what this is all about.'

'Please don't talk in riddles, Leon.'

'Well, if I'm to believe that you didn't do this on purpose, that fame wasn't top of your agenda when you agreed to work for me, then what else could possibly have induced you to say yes?' His eyes licked over her.

'I just told you. I'm passionate about the Rénards. I h⸮ve been since I was a child.' She avoided his gaze, ⸮ing it was only designed to humiliate her further. 'Is ⸮ard for you to believe?'

⸮he looked up he was staring at her with an intensity which told her there was nowhere to hide. 'It is when I know that for every minute you spend working on them you spend thirty thinking about me.'

Cally felt horror tear through every tissue in her body, not only because, to her shame, he was right and he knew it, but because she was terrified that what he implied was true. Had she accepted this job because the feelings he evoked in her obliterated everything else? No, she'd accepted it for the sake of her career, the Rénards.

'You're wrong, Leon.' Her voice was a husky whisper.

'Am I? Then how would *you* explain the symptoms. Dilated pupils, shallow breathing, the way you can't stop yourself from running your tongue over your lower lip every time you look at me? For someone who's supposed to be an expert on diagnosis and protection, I would have thought it was obvious.'

'I don't need protection,' Cally shot out determinedly, not noticing the look that flared in his eyes at her words.

'No, I didn't suppose for one minute that you would.'

But before she had time to process what he meant he slid his hand across her back and drew her to him, until their bodies were pressed so closely together that in the half light it would have been impossible for an onlooker to discern where she ended and where he began.

She froze, wanting to push him away, but unable to muster the strength. 'Leon, don't.'

He held perfectly still, save for his thumb tracing the base of her spine with an affectionate intimacy that made her want to cry out. 'Why not, *chérie,* when we both know it is what you want?'

Cally shook her head wretchedly. 'Be-because you don't want to.'

At her words even his thumb stopped moving and he regarded her with a faint look of surprise. 'Is it not obvious that I want you so much I have lost the ability to think straight?'

'But in London…'

He trailed his hand up her back and rested his fingers on the pulse beating wildly in her neck. 'It seems we were both a little guilty of saying one thing and meaning another in London.'

Her head fell back to look into his eyes, her own eyes widening as she realised that his were completely unflinching. He meant it. Though that ought to have changed nothing, to Cally it changed everything. He *did* desire her. Much as she'd been convinced that was impossible, much as she'd never dreamed she could ever feel such fervent need in return, suddenly it consumed her so overwhelmingly that she didn't even feel like the same Cally she had been two weeks ago. And, although she knew the safest option would be to button down her feelings as if they were nothing but awning caught in a disobedient wind, although she had never felt more terrified in her life, above all she understood that she would never know what it truly was to live unless she let it fly. Now.

'Leon, I—'

'Want me to kiss you again?' he ventured, moving his face so close to hers that his lips were only millimetres away.

The small sound that escaped from her throat said it all. It was unconscious, automatic, and with it he closed the gap between their mouths and gave an equally primal groan.

The kiss was exactly as she'd remembered but completely different at the same time. Not only did it feel like turning every cell in her body to liquid with each masterful stroke of his tongue, but now there was no languid music deciding their tempo, his hunger set the pace and dared her to match it. Not only did he smell of that distinctive musk she knew she would never fully be able to drive from her mind, it was now mixed with the smell of the sea—salty, damp and agonisingly erotic. So potent that she had to cling on to him to stop her knees from buckling. As she did, they stumbled forward a little, the heel of her shoe catching something other than floor.

Her eyes flew open to find it was the foot of an easel, and suddenly she remembered where they were and froze. 'The paintings!'

'Forget the damned paintings,' he drawled, steadying the fully clothed *Amour* with unconcerned ease. 'Let's go upstairs.'

The thought of the royal bedroom terrified Cally. Down here she could almost believe that he wasn't the prince, that she hadn't completely taken leave of her senses. She bit her lip for a moment, knowing that suggesting the alternative required a boldness she wasn't sure she possessed. But then she looked at him; his eyes were so hungry for her that it was almost possible to forget that she lacked anything at all. She swallowed down the excess of saliva that had formed in her mouth and imagined her fear disappearing with it. 'Actually, do you…do you mind if we stay here?'

The thought of taking her here and now made Leon harder than he had ever been in his entire life.

'Mind?' he breathed, doing nothing to disguise the roughness of his voice. 'The only thing I mind is that you are still wearing that dress.'

Cally's moment of relief was replaced by a new army of nerves. 'It does seem a little formal,' she whispered hesitantly as his hand trailed down her neck and swept around the circle of her breast. Instinctively she arched her back to encourage his hand upwards to the unbearable tightness of her nipple, but instead his fingers moved behind her, releasing the zip of her dress with ease and peeling the straps from her shoulders.

It was then that she remembered with horror the jade green basque and panties she was wearing underneath. She had put it on in that insane moment earlier when she'd been filled with delight at the thought of wearing the dress, followed by the girlish longing to try on the beautiful matching lingerie, the likes of which she had never worn in her life. It had felt so good, and, never supposing for a minute that anyone would see it, she'd seen no harm in keeping it on. Suddenly she felt ridiculous. What must he think of her, standing before him in lingerie that made her look like a courtesan at the Moulin Rouge, when she was nothing but an art restorer from Cambridge who hadn't had sex for almost a decade, and had never been good at it even then?

But when he peeled her dress down to her ankles and stepped back the pleasure on his face was so palpable—as if this was exactly how he had expected her to look, how she should look—that he made her feel like a butterfly emerging from a chrysalis. So much so that it was easy to forget how many other more beautiful, more experienced women than her must have stood before him like this. Easy to forget her old insecurities, to think only about how much he seemed to want her, how much she wanted him.

Cally reached forward with new-found boldness to encourage his T-shirt from his jeans.

'Allow me,' Leon interrupted, deftly removing both so that he was standing before her in nothing but his silky dark

boxers, every inch of hard muscle illuminated in the re-
fracted light from the lamp still lying on the floor like
some piece of modern art.

He pulled her to him with renewed urgency, and she
bucked in pleasure as at last his thumb brushed over her
nipple through the lace of the bodice, making her whole
body tremble.

'I hope you're not cold?' he asked, the corner of his
mouth quirking into a smile as he circled the taut peak.

'No.' She shook her head, her breathing ragged. 'Not *cold*.'

'Good,' he rasped, raising his arms and moving behind
her to slowly unlace the basque.

'Are you?' Cally whispered.

'Am I what?' he whispered distractedly as he kissed the
delicious hollow between her neck and her shoulder.

'Are you cold?'

'What do you think?' he ground out as the basque fell
to the floor and he spun her round to face him, revelling in
the sight of her.

Slowly, tentatively, she daringly reached out her hand
to touch him through the thin, silky fabric. 'You feel pretty
warmed up to me.'

Leon closed his eyes and groaned as she gradually
tugged down his boxers. When he opened them again her
eyes were fixed on him, her whole body momentarily still.

'What are you thinking?' he asked choppily.

Cally forced herself to blink, stunned by her own
boldness, by the size of him, by the way his scar led into
the mass of thick, dark curls. 'Your ego is big enough as it
is,' she breathed, suddenly nervous again.

'So, show me,' he teased in delight.

Cally looked into the depths of his eyes, her mind filling

with a host of unfamiliar and erotic images that she was convinced he must somehow be transmitting to her. Images which excited her even more than they surprised her, made her forget that she wasn't the kind of woman who instinctively understood the art of love, made her think quite the opposite. Slowly, slowly, with her breath caught nervously in her throat, she began to feather light kisses from beneath his belly button to the tip of his arousal.

Leon watched. Her breasts grazed the shafts of his thighs as she took him in her mouth. It was almost too much for him to bear. He guided her upwards and towards the sofa.

'I want to be inside you.'

Cally wanted him inside of her too, irrationally, inexplicably. In that instant she understood, however astonishing, that was what she had wanted from the very first moment she'd laid eyes on him. Now he was sitting on the sofa, guiding her legs to either side of him, his middle finger rushing up her inner thigh, finding the most intimate part of her, moist, open, *ready*.

She heard herself gasp in shock as he lowered her down onto him. Not in pain, she thought in amazement, but in pleasure. He was so warm, so thick, and it felt so right that Cally wondered how on earth she'd never known it could be like this before. Before she had time to examine what that meant, her thoughts faded like a watercolour in the rain as he began to rock her slowly back and forward.

'Now you,' he breathed hotly, slowing his pace and encouraging her to set the speed. Cally hesitated and then slowly began to move, heat rising through her. Leon placed his hands on her bottom, watching her.

'Close your eyes.'

Cally felt her breathing grow faster as she increased

pace, Leon suckling her breasts. An uncontrollable groan of pleasure broke from her throat. The sound shocked her into opening her eyes, and she slowed the pace fractionally.

'Let go,' he commanded.

'No, I…I don't know… I can't.'

'Yes, you can,' he replied forcefully, and she felt him shift slightly beneath her, reaching even deeper inside her, so deep, she felt her muscles contract around the hard length of him and the beginning of a new sensation that was so frighteningly powerful—like teetering on the edge of an unfamiliar precipice—that she didn't know what to do; she was afraid to let go.

'Now,' he urged, but still her eyes were squeezed tight. 'Damn you, I can't hold on!'

Cally felt his climax rip through him, saw the tendons in his neck go taut, felt his seed spill deep inside her, and…

It was only then, as she had been on the cusp of her very first orgasm, that she realised they hadn't used a condom.

CHAPTER SEVEN

HALF-WRAPPED in the maroon throw that covered the sofa, Cally felt instantly cold. No, cold was an understatement. She felt sub-zero, as though if she went anywhere near a thermometer the mercury would shrink in on itself and disappear altogether.

They hadn't used a condom.

She stared at the black restless sea outside the window, and then across at Leon, who lay by her side in a state of repose, thick-lashed eyes closed. How could they have been so stupid? They weren't a couple of naive teenagers, they were grown adults, for goodness' sake. He was a prince, for whom such basics had to be even more important than they were to the average male, and she was ordinarily so sensible that she never left the house without an umbrella and a packet of plasters. So why on earth hadn't either of them given a second thought to the small matter of protection?

Cally opened her mouth to share the burden of their irresponsibility, but just as she was about to speak a warning siren went off in her brain. *Protection.* She screwed up her eyes, their earlier conversation dropping back into her mind like bad news through a letterbox, her own words echoing back at her: *I don't need protection.*

Oh, dear God, he hadn't actually assumed that she'd meant the contraceptive kind, had he? No, he couldn't have. Perhaps Montéz was a pioneer of the male Pill and he hadn't thought to mention it. Or maybe, since he never intended to get married, he'd had the snip. Oh, who the hell was she trying to kid? She'd inadvertently led the most virile man she'd ever met to believe that she was protected, and it was a lie. And now there was every chance that his seed was already firmly rooted inside her.

Don't be so ridiculous, Cally, she reprimanded herself. *Whatever the movies would have you believe, the chances of getting pregnant after only one night are miniscule. Look at Jen—it took over a year of trying to get both Dylan and Josh. You're just a natural born worrier trying to punish yourself because for once in your life you acted a little recklessly.* Her eyes returned to Leon; his whole body was at ease in the aftermath of their lovemaking. What would be the good in telling him that he'd misinterpreted what she'd said? He'd probably laugh at her for being the faintest bit concerned. Either that, or he'd think she'd done it on purpose because she wanted to have his baby.

Cally untangled her legs and swung them over the edge of the sofa, horrified at the thought. Then she froze again. On some unconscious level, did she want his baby? Suddenly an idyllic image popped into her brain: Leon and her in the water teaching two children how to swim, a boy with dark blond hair like his father's, a girl with little red pigtails. Quickly, she forced herself to snap out of it. She didn't even like the man, and he no doubt took the same view of children as he did of marriage. Which was perfect, because she'd known for years that she was neither wife nor mother material, and that suited her just fine—even if at this precise moment she couldn't for the life of her remember why.

Because it allowed her to focus on her career, she recalled despondently, staring up at the paintings and then down at the rolled-up newspaper below them, remembering she had a whole other set of worries to occupy her mind on that front. Worries that were far more palatable than why she had never known making love could be that good until now, or why she wanted to crawl back into his embrace and stay there for as long as he'd have her.

Worries like whether she even still had a job, she thought, abruptly realising that she was still *sans* clothes, and that if she didn't think fast she was not only in serious danger of being fired but of being fired in the nude. The horrifying thought spurred her into action, and she quickly slipped from the sofa to locate her clothes, not noticing the way Leon's nostrils flared in arousal as he watched her dismiss the complicated hooks and ribbons of her underwear and throw on the dress without it.

Cally tiptoed across to where the newspaper lay pitifully beside the fallen lamp and picked it up. She took one more look at the offending page and then folded it away, trying not to think about how much she still wanted to scream at him for being so unreasonable. She understood now that it would do her no good.

Leon watched through heavy-lidded eyes as she reacquainted the light with its shade. Her hair was mussed from their lovemaking, her expression so misty-eyed that he was reminded of the first time he had seen her at the preauction. It seemed strange that he should be reminded of the moment he had suspected her of being the kind of woman to cloud things with emotion, when she had come

to him dressed to seduce. It was perfectly obvious that it
had all been an act, that what she really wanted was the kind
of no-strings affair she was no doubt accustomed to. After
all, why else would she be on the Pill, or have casually got
up to retrieve her dress, instead of trying to embrace him
afterwards, the way emotional women always did?

It didn't please him as much as it ought to have done.
Instead it made him wonder, irrationally, how many men
she had gone to like that, straddled and used the sum of her
obvious feminine wiles to get her own way with? Yet she
hadn't climaxed. For the first time in his life he was struck
by a momentary fear of sexual inadequacy, but he dismissed it just as quickly. She had been about to come, and
she had fought it on purpose. In some attempt to show him
that she was in control? he wondered angrily, irritated that
he hadn't been able to hold off his own orgasm.

'I will speak to Jen first thing in the morning, make sure
she understands the paintings should never have been mentioned,' Cally said quietly, feeling his eyes upon her. 'And
you have my word that I will never find myself in danger
of breaking your law again.'

A shadow darkened his face at the note of disapproval
in her voice. 'It's not *my* law. The royal family of Montéz
has always been forbidden territory to the press. And with
good reason. Being followed around like the stars in some
hideous reality TV show can only interfere with our work
on the island.'

'But your brother—'

'My brother upheld exactly the same law until he met
Toria.'

Cally raised her eyebrows and looked directly into his
eyes for the first time since she had moved away from the

sofa, disturbed as much by the discovery that a reasonable principle lay behind the law as by his glorious nudity. 'She got him to change it?'

'In a word, yes.' It didn't cure the look of curiosity on Cally's face. Leon drew in a short, frustrated breath, not sure why he felt so impelled to explain. 'Toria came to Montéz to star in a low-budget movie one summer when I was serving in the Marine Nationale. She had no talent, but she was desperate for fame and incredibly attractive. When she heard that the Crown Prince favoured a low profile over celebrity status, she thought it was preposterous and decided to seek him out. Girard was fifteen years her senior, lonely and flattered.'

He made a pattern with his fingernail on the arm of the sofa, not looking up. 'By the time of my next visit home, she had convinced him to marry her, and by the time of the wedding she had persuaded him that the media exposure was vital to her career. Which wouldn't have been so detestable if she had accepted even one role after he had given her the exposure she craved. She told him she was waiting for the right part, whilst all the time dragging him to photo shoots for magazines, movie premieres, A-list parties. All the time Montéz was suffering, and Girard was growing more and more exhausted. Eventually it came to a head.' Leon's expression turned as dark and foreboding as the night outside the window. 'They had been invited to a high-profile awards ceremony in New York on the same day as the private memorial service held annually to mark the anniversary of our mother's death. Toria demanded he go with her.' He looked stricken with guilt. 'I told him I would never forgive him if he did.'

'He went with her,' Cally breathed, recalling that the tragedy had taken place in the States.

'No. He decided to try and do both.' Leon gritted his
teeth, remembering that, for all his faults, Girard's peace-
keeping skills had been second to none. 'Toria went ahead
without him. He stayed for the memorial, vowing to meet
her at the awards ceremony as soon as he could. And he
would have made it—but he fell asleep at the wheel on the
stretch between JFK airport and the auditorium.' Leon's
eyes glazed with pain. 'When Toria called to give me the
news, all she could ask was why he hadn't been using a
chauffeur.'

'I'm sorry,' Cally whispered, wanting to tell him not to
blame himself, seeing in his eyes that he did. 'I had no idea.'

'Very few people did. Toria adored the press, and the
press adored her. After his death everyone wanted to interview the poor, grieving widow.' He gave a bitter, broken
laugh. 'It was the best performance of her career.'

Cally could only imagine what it must have been like
to deal with that in every newspaper and on every news
channel, having just lost his brother and been thrust into
the role of prince. 'So you reinstated the law?'

She saw him hesitate, and instantly his expression
became shuttered. 'It was around that time, yes.'

'And Toria?'

'Never forgave me for denying her the media circus
here in Montéz. So she moved to New York. She still turns
up occasionally with a mouthful of idle threats.'

'I'm sorry,' Cally repeated, understanding now why he
had automatically assumed that she wanted to use her work
here to feed off his fame, that she had planned the article.
Somehow, the revelation made her feel even closer to him
than she had done when they'd been making love. She
looked down at the newspaper she was still holding and

clutched it tighter. 'And I meant it when I said that nothing like this will ever happen again.'

She didn't see Leon's gaze drop to her hand, the look of distaste which shaped his mouth, as if he was a soldier who'd just realised he was inadvertently fraternising with the enemy. 'Good,' he replied, reaching for his jeans. 'Because as my mistress I require your absolute discretion.'

Cally's head jerked up in disbelief. 'Your *what?*'

'My mistress,' he said in a clipped tone which suggested he found having to repeat himself an inconvenience.

She stared at him in horror, suddenly feeling like a trapeze artist who thought she'd caught the bar in her hands but was suddenly plummeting towards the ground. 'And when exactly did I agree to be that?'

Leon shook his head. She *had* to be kidding. Surely she didn't expect him to buy the holier-than-thou charade now? 'I rather think your actions did the talking, don't you? Unless you're going to tell me that that little outfit and those moves are all part of some new and innovative conservation technique.' He dropped his head to one side. 'Although, it was certainly revitalizing, I'll give you that.'

The rant she'd been preparing collapsed under the weight of hurt and shame. 'No wonder you insist on never being quoted in the press. You're so crude, your people would question your royal blood.'

For a second an acute sharpness, almost a wince, cut across his face—but then as fast as it had come it was gone.

'I thought you liked your men to tell it like it is. Don't tell me sex has made you sentimental?'

'Hardly.' Cally turned away, fighting the tears that pricked behind her eyes.

'Then I suggest you spare me the lecture and come and have something to eat.'

'I'm not hungry.'

'Really?' he goaded. 'Or is it simply that you can't swallow that I was right all along?'

'Right about what?'

'That you only accepted this job because you wanted to go to bed with me.'

Cally's hurt caught fire, transforming into white-hot fury. 'Is your ego so gigantic that you can't accept that after years studying art restoration, and months of preparing to work on the paintings before we even met, that maybe *they* were the reason?'

'Of course I can accept that, *chérie*. All women who forge a career do so with gusto until they get whatever it is they really want. Fame, sex, whatever. Now you have sex, you may drop the pretence.'

'So, because your brother's wife was a manipulative bitch who wasn't interested in having a career once she'd seduced your brother, in your eyes the entire female population is guilty of the same crime?'

Leon raised one derogatory eyebrow at her hackneyed analysis. 'On the contrary, I've based my assumptions entirely on you. You'd barely touched the paintings before this little—how would you like me to phrase it delicately for you?—episode. And I hardly think touching *them* is your top priority now.'

Cally averted her eyes as he looked down at his body, as if he was remembering where she had trailed her hands, her lips. Why the hell had he still not put on his flaming T-shirt? 'They *are* my only priority, they always have been. Every job takes a while to settle into. You employed me because I am the best person to do it, and I still am. I'm not some virgin priestess who's lost her gift because I've lain with a man!'

'Oh, I think we both know you're not that, Cally, don't you?' he said silkily, his gaze raking over her with renewed desire. 'Just like I think we both know that your being capable of the job is only half the reason I employed you.'

'What?' Cally felt her whole body tense.

With a look of unconcern, Leon reached for his T-shirt. 'Don't sound so surprised, Cally. Do you suppose I employed you, despite the fact that you proved yourself indiscreet in London, purely because of your skills? I employed you for the same reason that you accepted—because we both knew that the sex between us would be *incroyable*.'

Cally wouldn't have thought it possible that her body could wind itself any tighter, but it did, so tight she felt faint. Clamminess broke out at the nape of her neck, between her breasts, behind her knees, heat pouring over her in a wave. It *had* been incredible, and it was incredible that he thought so too. But after everything she had worked for, fought for, clung to… He had only given her the job because he wanted to have sex with her? Cally felt sick. She had supposed there was no greater blow than the gallery losing the paintings that night at the auction, believed there was nothing more mortifying than his subsequent rejection, then discovering that he had lied. But this was even worse.

'I hate you.'

For a second Leon looked slightly taken aback. Only for a second. 'And yet you still desire me.' He shook his head condescendingly. 'Reason is always at such a disadvantage when paired with that.'

'Not any more,' she answered, willing it to be true. 'We shared an attraction, and we saw it through to its natural conclusion, but—'

'So that was the euphemism you were looking for.' He nodded slowly, as if she were one of a new species whose peculiar habits he was coming to learn. 'Attraction, natural conclusion…'

'But now it's over,' she concluded abruptly, catching sight of the Rénards. 'So, if you will just kindly confirm whether I may continue with my work…?'

'Do you really suppose that our shared *attraction* is something that has ceased to exist because we have given into it once?' He stalked across to where she was standing. 'Desire is an animal. We set it free, it cannot be tied up again.'

It can be, Cally thought. *It has to be.* She bit her lip, her mind traitorously filling with the erotic image of Leon tied up.

'Well, I'm sorry to disappoint you, but I think the animal has run off,' she said, so loudly that she gave herself away.

Leon laughed, the sound so deep and low it sent a vibration through her body. 'You still want to pretend you don't feel it, *chérie?* Be my guest, continue with your *work.* I give you a week at most before you're begging me to take you again, because if I don't you'll die of longing.' He stopped at the door, one eyebrow cocked. 'Unless, of course, you want to be done with the whole pretence and join me for dinner right now?'

'Like I said, I'm not hungry.'

'Of course you're not,' he mocked. 'Just like you weren't thirsty that night in London.' And with that he turned on his heel and left her once more.

* * *

Over the next few days Cally did everything she could to forget how it had felt to make love to Leon Montallier. She tried to excuse away that night as a single moment of recklessness she had simply been due for a while, like last February, when she'd got a sore throat and had conceded that she couldn't go any longer without succumbing to a winter cold. She relabelled her desire for him as nothing more than curiosity about his body which had now been satisfied. But, no matter how hard she tried, it was impossible not to think about the incredible way he'd made her feel, about the sensations which she'd never experienced before in all of her twenty-six years.

Which ought to have been crazy, because she wasn't a virgin. Yes, she might have only ever slept with one other man, but sex was sex, wasn't it? No, Cally thought, apparently it wasn't. What she'd just experienced with Leon had felt like exactly the kind of lovemaking she'd read about, whereas with David... Well, from the very first day he had talked her into it, she'd never really enjoyed their forays in the bedroom department. They had been rushed, uncomfortable, and had always left her feeling somehow inadequate—not least on the night when she had finally plucked up the courage to ask him if they could try kissing a bit more first, because she wasn't sure it felt exactly the way it was supposed to for her. He had told her not to be so absurd, and that if she didn't like it as it was then she was obviously just lacking the right gene.

In her naivety, she had always supposed she did lack something. Now she understood that she had simply been lacking the right sexual partner. But 'right' only in *that* sense, she thought grimly; Leon might have altered her perception on sex, but he'd confirmed that Prince Charming only existed in fairy tales. Which was why she had to forget him and get on with the paintings.

It felt a little like trying to push rocks through a sieve—never more so than during the hours in which he insisted on silently watching her work, as if it was an endurance test he was waiting for her to fail—but slowly, slowly, she began to make progress. In fact, after she had completed the cleaning of the first painting and begun work on the infill, she almost felt her old focus return. Almost, because to her surprise she found that, on the few occasions she became completely absorbed in the paint work, she would find herself drifting off into thoughts about two things in particular, neither of which were things she might have expected to find herself thinking about.

The first was that she was repeatedly and inexplicably struck with a burning desire to begin working on a painting of her own, to the extent that one afternoon, when she'd known she had the palace to herself, she had begun sketching the remarkable view from the studio window onto a piece of spare canvas. She didn't have the faintest idea why, because she hadn't painted anything of her own since her split from David, and it seemed incomprehensible that she should do so now when she was finding even her conservation work a struggle, but something impelled her to.

The second distraction was Leon, but not in the sexual way that haunted her whenever she closed her eyes. When she was busy on the paintings what she'd catch herself thinking about most frequently was the conversation they'd had immediately after their lovemaking, when he had told her about his brother. And to Cally that seemed even harder to forget. Aside from Leon revealing that his insistence against media attention wasn't just a dictatorial whim, she couldn't help wondering if it was significant that he, the man who insisted on such confidentiality, had told her something so private about his family. But, just as quickly as such thoughts came, she would dismiss them. After all, he had followed it up with the assumption that she would become his mistress, for goodness' sake, and it didn't come much more meaningless than that. Besides, even if they had been in some parallel universe and his *doppelgänger* had declared it was significant, she'd walk away anyway. Wouldn't she?

Cally's eyelids fluttered down to meet her cheeks in a moment of mortification as she envisioned turning back and walking willingly into his arms. But that was just because in the parallel universe he'd be the complete opposite of who he was, not a heartless prince, not a lying bastard, she told herself at the exact moment he entered the room, sending a shiver of awareness down her spine.

'I'm actually on a really tricky bit. Do you mind not watching today?' she said quickly without turning around.

'You mean I'm in danger of distracting you?' he drawled.

'Not specifically you—anyone,' Cally lied, only hoping he hadn't guessed that when he watched her it felt like every movement she made was being magnified and projected on the wall for his scrutiny.

'If you say so. As it happens, I've only come to tell you that Kaliq and his fiancée will be joining us for dinner this evening, so you'll need to be ready by eight.'

Cally blanched. When they had been unable to make it on Saturday she'd known he planned to reschedule, but it hadn't occurred to her again since… Since he'd made it clear that asking her to join them last time had had nothing to do with her expertise and everything to do with wanting her to become his mistress.

'Actually, I planned to begin work on the nude this evening. I'm almost finished on this one.' They both turned to the first painting, as surprised as each another to see that the restoration work was almost complete, and the difference it made was breathtaking.

'Well, then, it seems the perfect place to stop, does it not?'

'All the same, I'd rather not join you for dinner.'

'Then it's a good job it's not optional, then, isn't it?'

Cally glowered at him. 'Since I declined the generous offer of becoming your mistress, I rather think it is up to me when and with whom I dine.'

'Not if it is a requirement of your job, which, for your information, is the capacity in which I require you to be there.'

'Really? Since my job is only to restore and conserve art, am I to assume that the prince is bringing a painting with him that you'd like me to take a look at between courses, perhaps?'

'Kaliq does not share my passion for art,' he growled.

'Then how can my joining you for dinner possibly be in the capacity of work?'

'The meeting is part business, part pleasure.'

'Well, then, why do you need me when you're the expert on combining the two?'

A cloud settled over his features. 'Kaliq and I have a trading treaty to discuss, but I also wish to toast my acquisition of the paintings.'

'Like a new Ferrari or a penthouse in Dubai,' she said sarcastically. 'So I can't understand why you'd want me there to lower the tone.'

'That's because you have no idea how good you look

in that green ensemble,' he ground out beneath his breath. 'But luckily your comprehension isn't a requirement. I am your employer, and I consider your presence tonight a necessary part of your work. And, since I am not asking you to do anything more unpalatable than have a world-class meal in more than amicable company, I cannot comprehend *your* objection. Unless, of course, you are worried that you might not be able to keep your desire tied up when you see me in a dinner suit.'

'God, you're arrogant!'

'So you *do* think you can keep it tied up?'

'Of course I—I have no desire for you!'

'Then we don't have a problem, do we? I will see you at eight. Oh, and wear the green dress, won't you?'

'Over my dead body.'

'Why, does it bring back too many memories?' He raised his eyebrows, daring her to say no.

She stared back, mute, furious.

'Good. Eight it is, then.'

CHAPTER EIGHT

RESISTING the urge to storm into her room and find out why the hell she wasn't ready yet, Leon paced the forecourt of the palace and turned his thoughts to his guests, whom Boyet had gone to collect from Kaliq's villa. After years of failing to convince his oldest friend to bring a female companion to Montéz, he could scarcely believe that tonight Kaliq would be accompanied by his future bride. Leon shook his head. Despite the law of Kaliq's homeland, which stated he had to marry in order to inherit the throne, Leon had never really believed that the cool and cynical sheikh would settle down. In fact, when he had first received word of his engagement, Leon had dismissed it as rumour. Then, when Boyet had confirmed it, he had supposed that in the wake of his father's ill health duty must have forced Kaliq to find a docile Qwasirian bride. So discovering that his choice was in fact a British model had filled Leon with both surprise and concern. A concern which on second thoughts was unnecessary, because Leon knew that Kaliq, unlike Girard, was an astute judge of character and would never marry a woman who wouldn't make a perfect queen and mother to his children.

Leon stopped pacing, wondering if the concern in his

chest might therefore really be for himself, for Montéz. No doubt before long Kaliq would have an heir to his throne. He drew in a deep breath, wondering how long he could go on ignoring his own duty—the duty which should never have been his, he thought grimly. What happened if Toria's body clock started ticking in the meantime? No, he thought, pacing the floor and wishing he had time to tear off his clothes and obliterate those thoughts in the ocean. She didn't have a maternal instinct in her body. It wouldn't happen, and he was only allowing it to bother him because for the past three days he'd been driven wild by her red-haired equivalent.

Cally. Leon's body tightened beneath the tailored fabric of his suit at the thought of her. The rational part of his brain warned him that she was every bit as conniving as his sister-in-law—and ought to be just as unappealing. Except in his mind they couldn't be further apart. Toria had offered herself to him on a plate more times since Girard's death than he cared to remember, but he found the thought of her about as desirable as walking into the web of a black widow spider. Yet Cally…

How many times over the past few days had he gone into that studio and had to leave because if he'd stayed a moment longer he would have ripped the damned paintbrush out of her hand and kissed her until she begged him to make love to her again? So many times he wished he could forget. Was it some kind of elaborate game to ensure his surrender to her was total, helpless? If it was, then it was futile. No matter how many cold showers it took to keep his permanent state of semi-arousal at bay, he would be patient, and he would have her on *his* terms. It was only a matter of time until she came to him again and admitted

that he was what she had wanted all along. And, if her resistance to this evening's meal had been anything to go by,
it would be soon.

'Sheikh A'zam and Miss Weston are here, Your
Highness,' Boyet announced, heading towards him.

'Thank you. Right on time.'

It was a shame he couldn't say the same about Cally,
Leon thought, his nostrils flaring.

Cally stared at the jade green dress hanging on her wardrobe door. He had her cornered. If she didn't go to dinner,
not only would she miss the opportunity to share her work
on the paintings, and be placing her job in jeopardy for a
second time, but he would also deduce it was because she
thought herself incapable of resisting him. The dilemma
with the dress was just as bad. Wear something else, and
he'd know it meant something to her. Wear it as he'd
demanded, and she might just as well have agreed to
become his mistress. But then he'd chosen everything in
her wardrobe anyway, she thought sullenly.

Aware that she had been cutting it fine when she'd left
the studio at seven-thirty, and that she'd now been staring at
the dress for what felt like an age, Cally glanced at her
watch. Seven fifty-five. She tried to ignore the usual sense
of horror she felt at the prospect of making anyone wait on
the rare occasions she was late. So what if she was late for
him? He could hardly get annoyed that she had been working
late to finish the restoration of the first painting for his guests
to see. But it would be mortifying to make *them* wait, Cally
thought suddenly, grasping for the dress. After all, they were
what this whole evening was about. He wasn't even part of
the equation. All she had to do was remember it.

* * *

'Ah, Cally.' Leon turned to watch her descend the stairs with a sardonic expression. 'You decided to join us.'

'I wasn't aware I had a choice,' Cally hissed under her breath, before smiling broadly at his guests, grateful to have an excuse to take her eyes off of the disarming sight of him in his navy dinner suit.

'May I introduce His Royal Highness Sheikh Al-Zahir A'zam, and his fiancée, Miss Tamara Weston. Kaliq, Tamara, this is Cally Greenway.'

'It's a pleasure to meet you,' Cally said genuinely as she shook their hands, grateful that, although the sheikh was just as regal as she had imagined, and Tamara was stunning in an evening gown of mesmerising coral, they weren't the least bit disparaging towards her.

'Do you live here on Montéz?' Tamara asked her amiably as they took their seats at the antique dining table.

'I am just working on the island at the moment—'

'Cally is living here at the palace,' Leon interrupted. 'One of her many talents is restoring fine art. She is working on some paintings I purchased in London.' He looked directly at Kaliq. 'Rénard's *Mon Amour par la Mer*.'

Cally stared at him, so incredulous that he had cut her off that she didn't notice the significant look which Kaliq gave him in return. 'Congratulations, Leon. You must be very pleased.'

'It sounds fascinating. I'd love to see,' Tamara added, too polite to show that she had noticed Leon's rudeness.

'I'd be delighted to show you,' Cally replied, before Leon halted any elaboration on her part by bombarding Tamara with questions about their stay on the island, and cracking open the champagne to celebrate their engagement. And who could blame him? Cally thought as a plethora of palace staff she'd never seen before brought in platters of meats, cheeses, olives and fresh bread. Although Leon spoke to Tamara with appropriate respect, he was no doubt as captivated by her beauty as any man would be.

As captivated as you are by him, Cally thought despondently, unable to stop her eyes from straying to his mouth, or the lance of jealousy which jabbed at her heart.

'You must be used to exploring different countries by yourself?' She made the effort to chip into the conversation as Tamara mentioned that she had visited the university today whilst Kaliq had been working.

She nodded. 'I don't get as much time as I would like to explore when I am on a shoot abroad, but I don't mind travelling alone.'

'It sounds very exciting,' Cally replied with genuine admiration, trying to feel inspired by the possibilities that might await her once she had finished the Rénards. The kind of opportunities she'd spent a lifetime dreaming about but which suddenly seemed to have lost their appeal, she thought bleakly. She wondered how much longer she could go on pretending that was what she wanted when, in spite of all the reasons why she shouldn't, all she really wanted was for Leon to make love to her again more than she had ever wanted anything in her life.

'It can also be very dangerous.' Kaliq cut into the conversation. 'Naturally, once we are married Tamara will give up work, so it shall cease to become a concern.'

Cally registered the triumphant look on Leon's face and hated him for it. She could just imagine him adding Tamara's name to the list in his mind which proved that women only troubled themselves with a career until they secured themselves a position as a mistress or a wife. But he was wrong. She might have only just met them both, but it was obvious that the desert prince had only said that because he cared for Tamara with such a passion he couldn't bear the thought of her being at any kind of risk. And she only had to take one look at Tamara's less-than-impressed expression to know she would never let her future husband stop her if she chose to continue with her career.

What would it be like to be here because she mattered to Leon the way Tamara mattered to Kaliq? Cally thought hopelessly as the conversation moved on to discussing the forthcoming wedding. What would it be like to have a man love you so deeply that he wanted to spend his life with you, and who actually cared, not just about having you in his bed, but about your safety and well-being?

She didn't have a clue, and for the first time since David had quashed her dreams she couldn't think of anything worse than never finding out. But they were just childish dreams, she reminded herself as she pushed the main course of duck around her plate, and that was why she'd given them up. So why did it seem so difficult to go back to accepting that she was destined to be alone, the way she had been before she'd met him?

Because he had made her aware of the gaping hole in her life, she thought wretchedly as she watched him speak animatedly about the international trading treaty with Kaliq, shamefully aware that, though she had spent the past few days telling herself to forget how it had felt to make love to him, tonight she was failing more spectacularly than ever.

She drew in a ragged breath. If she gave in now she may as well toss her self-respect out with the trash. *He wants you as a mistress, nothing more,* she repeated in her mind. *And you don't even like him.* But as she listened to him chatting about his plans for the university, for cutting taxes, for strengthening the links between Montéz and Qwasir, even disliking him was getting more difficult. She had turned up here believing that, like David and the rest of his moneyed family, the ruler of Montéz was a snob who didn't care about anyone but himself. But there was no denying that Leon had his people's best interests at heart and that, palace and paintings aside, he also seemed remarkably frugal for a billionaire. Apart from one cleaner and the additional staff he had called upon tonight, Boyet seemed to be his only aide, and his pleasures, like diving out at sea, were equally simple. So how was she supposed to focus on hating him when the reasons for doing so were getting fewer by the second?

Because, prince among men or not, the stonking great reason remains: he only wants you to warm his bed. And if you give in to your desire now what does that say about you? That you have no pride, she answered inwardly. *Or you're so delusional that, in spite of all the evidence, you've started to believe in the fairy tale again.*

Either way, Cally knew that to give in to her desire would be to set herself up for a fall, but that didn't make it any easier to step away from the edge. Her whole being seemed attuned only to filling the gaping hole he had opened, she realised as she cracked open the hard layer of caramel on her crème brûlée and stole a glance at him. And she was unable to stop herself from wondering whether, when he looked at Kaliq and Tamara, their evident love for one another made him aware of a missing link in his own future too.

'Thank you, Leon, that was delicious.' Tamara's words made Cally snap out of her lust-induced daze.

Leon turned to Tamara. 'I hope you will persuade Kaliq not to leave it so long between visits in future.'

Tamara nodded.

'So long as you promise to visit Qwasir soon so that we can return the favour,' Kaliq added.

'What an excellent idea,' Leon said, eyeing Cally with increased hunger as he imagined making love to her in the sultry climes of the desert. 'Now, you must forgive us, but I find that tonight *I* am now somewhat exhausted.'

Leon, exhausted? Cally had no idea what he was playing at, but she knew that was impossible. She'd seen him get back from a fourteen-hour day of negotiations on the mainland only to dive straight into the ocean. Not that she had been watching out of her window to see when he got back or anything, she argued inwardly, then wondered who on earth she was trying to kid.

'I thought perhaps Sheikh A'zam and Tamara would like to see the paintings before they leave.'

'Well, that will be an additional incentive for them both to return.' Leon smiled through clenched teeth.

'But—'

He signalled over her shoulder for Boyet to bring the car round and shook his head. 'It won't be necessary, Cally, thank you.'

Cally could barely hide her fury as the two princes embraced and all four of them exchanged farewells, before Leon accompanied Kaliq and Tamara down the steps amidst well wishes for their nuptial plans.

When he returned she was standing at the top of the steps, hands on her hips.

'So you're done with even pretending my presence here tonight had to do with work? The boast that the Rénards were yours might have been enough of an ego boost for you, but surely the least you could do was have me show them to your guests? But, no, you bundle them away before it's even eleven o'clock. I'm not sure I've ever met anyone so rude.'

'There will be another time. I don't consider it rude when two people can't keep their hands off each other and clearly want to be alone.'

Cally smarted, forced to concede his insightfulness. 'They did seem very much in love.'

Leon looked her straight in the eye. 'I wasn't talking about them.'

She flushed crimson and broke his gaze. 'Then you have not only acted without manners but you have also misread this situation.'

'Have I?' he breathed, taking a step so disturbingly close that she had to shut her eyes to block out the sight of him. Except she could still sense him there, smell that unmistakable musk, which tonight was mixed with a citrusy cologne.

'Yes, just like you read everything wrong! That look on your face when Kaliq said that Tamara was giving up work—you think it proves your archaic theory about women using their career until they ensnare a man, then giving it up the second they've succeeded, but you're wrong. Kaliq simply cares about her safety.'

'So now you think you know my oldest friend better than me?'

'Don't you think it's possible for two people with their own careers to meet, fall in love and marry?' Cally cried, wondering whether she was asking the question of him or herself.

Leon gritted his teeth. There was that word again:

marriage. The one she allegedly loathed as much as him. *Allegedly.* 'Do you want me to say yes so that you have something to dream about, *chérie?*'

'I just—' Cally exhaled deeply. 'Aren't you ever worried the endless line of women will come to an end? That you'll end up alone?'

His face turned to thunder. 'Alone suits me fine.'

'I know.' She breathed deeply, trying to focus on one of the regal gold buttons on his jacket, and willing her feet to walk her away from him. But as she raised her eyes to his impossibly handsome face, bathed in the soft lights from the palace, her pride somehow felt like an inevitable sacrifice. Her fight had already gone—left at the bottom of her glass in the Road to Nowhere, lost down the back of the sofa in the studio, gone from the palace with Tamara and Kaliq.

Her voice was a whisper. 'I know, and I thought it suited me too. But I don't want to be alone tonight.'

CHAPTER NINE

IT SEEMED that admitting he couldn't bear to be alone even for one night was too much to ask of Leon Montallier. But, though Cally was well aware that her track record for reading the opposite sex was abysmal, she couldn't shake the feeling that his expression said it for him. In fact, if she hadn't known better, she would have sworn from the grim set of his mouth that she'd just stumbled upon his Achilles' heel. But, as he lightly brushed his hand down her side and resolutely scooped her up into his arms, all she knew was that he wanted her body with the same voracious need that she wanted his, and suddenly that felt like the only thing that mattered.

'This time we're going to do this properly,' he instructed her huskily as he carried her back into the palace and up an unfamiliar spiral staircase.

Unfamiliar, because this was the staircase that led to the master bedroom. Where, unlike in the studio, there could be no more pretending that this was somehow to do with the paintings, no more conveniently imagining that he was just an ordinary man, a diver in the Marine Nationale. He was the sovereign prince, and this was his palace. Perhaps it ought to have felt terrifying, yet somehow, as they entered the room with its stained-glass windows and four-poster bed, it felt utterly liberating. It was as if she'd had an internal pair of scales which she had been trying desperately hard to balance ever since she had arrived and finally she had let them tip. But, rather than the disaster she had felt sure would assail her, she felt a great surge of relief.

'I've been wanting to do this all night,' he breathed, lowering his head and releasing her just enough for her feet to touch the gold-and-aquamarine rug, whilst keeping her so tightly pressed to him she could feel the lines of his suit imprinted on her body through the thin fabric of her dress.

'Just all night?' she whispered against his lips, so provocatively that for a moment she wondered whether she was possessed by the spirit of some other woman, a woman who wasn't convinced that any minute now she'd lose her nerve, a woman who was confident—sexy, even. She realised that, without being wholly conscious of it, every time he touched her she became that woman. A woman she didn't recognise, but who she had always wanted to be.

'What do you think?' he bit out raggedly, answering her with an urgent, drugging kiss and reaching behind her, cupping her bottom, then running his hand down the back of her thigh, balling the dress in his hand.

Cally kissed him back with equal need, snaking her arms behind his back, encouraging the jacket from his shoulders until it fell to the floor.

Leon broke away from her momentarily, his eyebrow quirked at the exact same angle it had been the day he'd walked into the studio brandishing the hacked-off fabric of her jeans. 'You know, I've never met a woman who has so little regard for designer clothes.'

'Is that such a bad thing?' she whispered.

'On the contrary,' he answered roughly, 'right now I find it a very good thing.' And before Cally knew what was happening he reached his hands inside the neck of the jade green dress and pulled, tearing the garment in half and leaving her standing there in nothing but her own plain black bra and knickers.

He eyed them with a puzzled expression. 'That's not the underwear I selected.'

'No,' Cally said, her tone cautious but not without a note of defiance. 'It's not.'

Ever since that night she had steered clear of the tempting drawer full of lingerie and had repeatedly laundered her own set of smalls, not only because they were more comfortable to wear during the day but because she'd decided they were far more likely to prevent her thoughts from wandering than the feel of lace against skin. *Wrong again,* a voice chimed inside her head, but as she caught his gaze sliding over her with lust-filled appreciation it couldn't have felt more right.

'Is it a problem?' she asked, slanting him a daring look as she watched his pupils dilate.

'That depends.' Leon took a step back, drinking her in. 'On what?'

'On how good the show is,' he answered huskily, extending his arm, and she realised that his step backwards had put him in reach of a CD player.

Her legs almost buckled as she heard the slow, familiar beat begin to fill the room.

'Mississippi in the middle of a dry spell…'

It couldn't be a coincidence; it was their song. No, that was far too sentimental. It was the song that had happened to be playing that night. But what was it doing on the CD player in his bedroom if it didn't mean something to him too?

'Don't tell me,' she whispered, trying to make her voice sound light, 'you and Kaliq often meet up in dodgy rock bars, and there's one in the centre of Montéz called *La Route à*…'

'La Route à Nulle Part,' he said slowly, sexily, a smile tugging at his lips as she attempted the French for Road To Nowhere. 'Almost. Either that, or for some reason I couldn't get the damned song out of my head and I had to hear it again.'

'And did it work?' Cally asked, trying not to tremble as she slowly began to move in time with the music.

Leon's throat went dry as he watched her. 'Did what work?'

'Did it help you get it out of your head?'

'No.'

Cally felt her heart turn over. She wanted to bottle that feeling—the helplessness in his voice, that one syllable which told her she affected him as deeply as he affected her—but she dared not let him see.

'It is a memorable song,' she whispered.

'Very, very memorable.' He nodded as she daringly slipped down one strap of her bra.

'Has anyone—' he cleared his throat, his voice coming out so low it was almost inaudible '—has anyone ever told you how sexy you are?'

'Once,' she smiled, remembering Leon's warm breath in her ear on the dance floor. Tonight she even believed it. So much so that somehow, she—bookish, bad-at-sex Cally—had the confidence to strip in front of him in his royal chamber.

'Then I think you need telling some more. Because you are the sexiest woman I've ever known.'

And I've known a lot, was the unspoken, implicit end

of that sentence. But she didn't care, because his words were so precious to her that tonight it felt like they were the only two people in the world.

'So would you like it if I did this?' she asked innocently, hooking her thumbs into the sides of her knickers.

'Mmm.'

'Or this?' Cally teased, sliding her hands back up her sides and behind her to the catch of her bra. His eyes were transfixed by the sight of her breasts strained against the thin fabric.

'I've changed my mind,' he said in a clipped voice, and for a minute Cally froze, terrified this was going to be a repeat of that moment in the taxi. But her fears vanished as he quickly closed the gap between them. 'I'm through with waiting.'

Without a moment of hesitation he raised one hand behind her and unclasped her bra, tossing it to the floor to join the tatters of her dress. Her knickers went the same way.

'Perfect,' he breathed, his fingers taking the same path up her body as hers had done until he found her full, heavy breasts.

'Not quite!' she cried breathlessly.

'No?' he murmured against her skin, trailing a line of kisses along the base of her throat, his lips a whisper away from taking her nipple in his mouth.

'No! No. I…I want you naked with me.' Her fingers moved to his shirt, fumbling with the buttons.

'*Now* you decide to be more careful, *chérie?*' he scolded.

Cally pulled back, and, comprehending what he inferred, shook her head with a thrill. But, just as she dropped her eyes to his shirt to ponder how, his hands had covered hers and they were ripping open his shirt, buttons flying in all directions until he was naked from the waist up, every inch of his torso revealed in all its golden glory.

Quickly he pulled her back to him so that her breasts were crushed against the hardness of his bare chest, and with equal speed she reached for the waistband of his trousers. In a second he had discarded them and was standing there in nothing but his dark navy boxers, which did nothing to hide his straining excitement.

But, if Cally had thought their mutual urgency was a sign that their lovemaking was to be as frantic as three nights ago, she was mistaken. As he led her towards the bed and slowly laid her down, she understood that when he'd said they were going to do this properly, he hadn't just meant that this time their lovemaking would take place in bed. Because, although she could see that his body was most certainly ready, his expression told her that he fully intended to explore her as if this was the very first time.

And in a way, as she watched him lick across her nipple with his tongue, the lines of his face taut with desire, it felt like it was. Because it was the only time she had ever truly given in to this kind of pleasure. It was as if until this moment her mind had always been a barren wasteland filled only with fears, but now in its place was a lush and tropical garden with no space for anyone but him. Him, the part of her she'd never known was missing, that she needed to complete her, to fill her.

'Leon!' She threw back her head as his fingers reached lower, dipping inside her. She squeezed her eyes tightly shut, riding the rhythmic sensation of his circling, intimate caress, reaching out to stroke her hand along his silky-smooth length, guiding it towards her. So hard, so virile…

Then suddenly her eyes flew open.

'What is it?' he bit out, afraid that she was going to choose this moment to have an attack of conscience.

'I—we need to use protection.'

Leon frowned. 'I thought you were on the Pill.'

Cally looked up at the ceiling, avoiding his gaze. 'I...I was, but...but, as I didn't expect to be here so long, I've run out.'

Leon shrugged, the momentary tension in his upper body released. 'No problem.'

As he reached across to the drawer of the bedside cabinet, Cally felt a hideous sense of shame wash over her. Not only because she had lied, but because his trust in her was so implicit that he hadn't thought to doubt her explanation for a second.

But as she felt the heat of his thighs parting her own, her mind returned to the tropical paradise, and she let go of her guilt. It was a misunderstanding that would have no consequence, an omission of the truth that he of all people would understand if it ever came to light. Which it wouldn't, she assured herself, as her body parted to welcome him.

Cally slid her fingers up his back and lost them in his hair, loving the feel of his body on top of hers as he entered her. She didn't have a clue how many perfect minutes passed as he moved slowly, assuredly, inside her, determined that they should both savour every second. She could see from the muscle in his jaw that he was fighting to keep his excitement on a leash, and she loved that most of all.

'Do you want to change position?' she asked, pretending she couldn't see that he wanted to up the tempo.

'No.' His voice was throaty. 'This time it's going to happen to you, and I want to watch.'

Once Cally might have blushed, tensed, vowed it was impossible—or possibly all three. Not tonight.

'Then take me a little faster,' she whispered.

Leon's eyes flared in pleasure as he did as she commanded. 'Tell me what else you like.'

'You,' she answered without thinking. 'Everywhere.'

Finding the only part of their bodies that wasn't already interlocked, Leon entwined her fingers with his, and if Cally had been clinging to one remaining sliver of control that was the moment she lost it. For with the tenderness of that gesture she gave in to the mounting sense of longing that felt like an intense pain but without any of the hurt, gave in to every exquisite stroke, each one more insistent than the last, like waves against a breakwater about to give way.

She heard a moan escape from her mouth, low, insistent, infused with pleasure. She felt him grow even harder within her at the sound, and then completely withdraw before deliciously filling her with a thrust that was thick and fast.

'Oh God!'

Cally felt the imaginary breakwater give way as every inch of her body was flooded with an exquisite heat, all-consuming, astonishing. The tide drew back and then washed over her again in a flurry of aftershocks as Leon cried out, reaching the height of his own pleasure just seconds after her own.

He'd been holding off, she realised, had wanted her to come first. It could have been to prove his own prowess, or to demonstrate that any restraint on her part was a thing of the past. But right at that moment as she lay locked in the circle of his arms she believed it was simply because he wanted her to know that pleasure. A pleasure she had never dreamed she was capable of reaching. Whatever happened, she would always be grateful for that.

'Thank you,' she whispered, shifting her body to his side, though her arm remained slung across his chest.

'You're welcome,' he smiled. 'I'm glad I managed to persuade you to give in to it.'

She wasn't sure whether he was talking about her desire for him or her orgasm. Perhaps it didn't matter.

'It was my first.'

Leon blinked in astonishment, observed the slash of colour still high on her cheekbones and the faint surprise in her bewitching green eyes, and felt a surge of triumph accompanied by a slow dawning of something unpleasant he couldn't quite put his finger on. So she hadn't been holding back that first time to prove a point; she simply hadn't recognised the sensation or known how to let go. Which meant nothing, he quickly rationalised, refusing to revisit the thought which had momentarily flashed across his mind when he'd seen her modest underwear. Her usual encounters were probably one-night affairs after a quick fondle on a darkened dance floor, that was all.

'It can take time to get to know a sexual partner,' he said, too patronisingly for Cally's liking.

'If you are implying my sexual history consists of one-night stands, then you're mistaken.' She bristled, moving away from him and tugging the sheet around herself so that there was something more substantial than air between them. He was steering the conversation down a road she didn't want to take, but she couldn't bear the thought of him thinking that way about her.

Leon hesitated, as if unable to decide whether asking the question that hovered on the tip of his tongue was really such a good idea. 'Then perhaps you'd care to fill me in with the correct history.'

'Not really.'

'I am a modern man, Cally. The women with whom I choose to share my bed have inevitably had other lovers. It is not something which concerns me.' At least, usually it wasn't.

'Well, then, I'm afraid my sexual CV is going to be unimpressive in comparison,' she said quietly, not wanting to think about his other lovers, and at the same time wishing he did give a damn whether or not she was a complete whore or not. 'There was only one other man before you.'

Leon's eyes widened in shock, and then the blinding satisfaction of the revelation gave way to something far less palatable: the short stab of his conscience as the truth slotted into place. The day he'd seen her at the pre-auction, the plain underwear... She wasn't some practised seductress who had set out to ensnare him, she was as good as innocent. Suddenly he felt consumed with regret for the assumptions he had made, the wrong he had done her.

And, ashamed though he was to admit it, worst of all he supposed he had always known on some level that she was the sentimental kind. He had simply chosen to believe the opposite rather than stick to his own rule. The rule that, in spite of everything, he wanted to break all over again.

'So who was he?' Leon propped himself up on his arm and looked at her. 'A fiancé?' He paused. 'A husband?'

Cally shook her head. 'No, David was never in any danger of finding himself in either of those categories when it came to me.'

'But you hoped so?'

She nodded reluctantly. 'But I should have known from the start that I lacked the right credentials.'

Leon's mouth was a picture of disdain. 'How do you mean?'

'He was the son of an earl. I was working part-time on his father's estate. I don't know why I persisted in thinking that the difference in class between us was irrelevant. My parents, I suppose.' She gave a brittle laugh. 'They always told Jen and me that there were no barriers.' She shook her head. 'They were wrong. It was nothing more to him than an affair with a scullery maid would have been to one of his ancestors. I let him talk me into sleeping with him because he told me he loved me—and, worse, I let him talk me out of continuing with my degree because he said going it alone would make me a better artist. He lied. One of the other girls working there warned me that David shared his father's misogynistic views on women of a certain class trying to better themselves by getting too much education, but I thought she was just jealous. Until I left uni, turned up on his doorstep and found out that he had got himself engaged to an heiress without bothering to tell me.'

Cally looked up and, seeing from the look in his eyes that she was in danger of being at the receiving end of his pity, she continued quickly. 'So, do you always quiz women about their ex-lovers in bed?'

'Only when they tell me I am the first man to make them reach orgasm,' Leon answered, filled with a new and grim understanding.

'To bolster your ego?'

'Because it's a shame, Cally. Fantastic sex is like…art.'

'You mean everyone should enjoy it, like putting a great painting in a public gallery?'

'Touché.' He raised one eyebrow sexily. 'No. I mean the more you learn, the more you enjoy it.'

And the more likely you are to see weaknesses in the work of an inexperienced artist, Cally thought dismally, realising that if her lack of sexual expertise hadn't said it for her then her attack of verbal diarrhoea had just given the impression that she only ever slept with men who she saw as potential husbands.

'I was very young then,' Cally added quickly. 'When I thought I wanted to marry David, I mean. Of course, I was upset by what happened, but I realised very quickly that I was not cut out to be anyone's wife.'

Leon eyed her with a degree of scepticism. 'And yet you say you do not wish to be a mistress either. That makes for a very cold life, Cally.' He ran his hand over her bare arm. 'And, if you are planning on pretending that you are a cold person, don't bother, because we both know different.'

She had resigned herself to the fact that her life was destined to be cold, Cally thought, only now aware of how sad that sounded. But that was because she'd never known this kind of passion, a passion she knew she couldn't fight anymore even if it was destined to go nowhere.

She shook her head. 'No, I'm not going to pretend that. But nor do I want to downgrade my role of art restorer to mistress.'

Cally saw a nerve work at his jaw. 'I shall presume that was a slip of the tongue and you meant *up*grade.'

'Don't. I take great pride in working hard to earn my own living, difficult as that might be for *you* to comprehend. I don't want to toss it in so I can be at your beck and call, have you tell me what to wear and when.'

'So what is it you *do* want?'

Leon wondered if he had heard himself correctly. Since when did he conduct affairs where he invited a woman to lay down the ground rules? Never, he thought, looking at her fiery red hair spilling across his pillow. But then never before had he ever experienced a desire which felt like it would render him permanently debilitated unless it was appeased. Or been so conscious that here was the last woman in the world who needed a man riding roughshod over her a second time, he thought ruefully. Maybe it was breaking his own rule, but so long as she meant what she said about not wanting to be anyone's wife there was no problem, was there?

'I want to carry on working here—under the terms we have already agreed—and I want this…' She scrambled around for a word which described whatever 'this' was, and decided that there wasn't one. 'This sex between us to be something entirely separate. That isn't about anything other than mutual pleasure because the opportunity, whilst I am here, exists.'

'Just like I can dive into the sea because it is outside my back door?' Leon ventured.

'Exactly.' Cally nodded, not knowing why that made her heart sink, when having him agree to treat this as a pleasure they both chose to indulge in was far more preferable to being made to feel like a call girl on extended loan.

'Good,' Leon replied abruptly, having heard exactly the answer he needed. 'Then you shall work during the day and share my bed at night.' He made a show of picking up his watch from the bedside table. 'Which, if I'm not mistaken, still gives us another eight and a half hours.'

And with that he tossed aside the sheet and pulled her to him all over again.

CHAPTER TEN

WHEN Leon had compared fantastic sex to art, Cally hadn't considered it as anything other than a boast about his sexual prowess. But in the weeks that followed she couldn't help thinking that there was more to his statement than even he would have given himself credit for. After the physical abandon of that night, she felt fundamentally altered, as if up until that point her life had been the equivalent of a rather dull and dreary still life, and now he had splashed it with vibrant colour.

As bright and vivid as the underwater paradise beneath them, Cally thought happily as she lay flat on the deck of his boat after an hour just spent snorkelling, breathing in the scent of sun cream and feeling the droplets of seawater evaporate off of her skin. Although she had insisted that she would work during the day, and only share his bed at night, Leon tended to leave the palace early in the morning and return just after lunch, and since it suited her to work to a similar pattern their afternoons were invariably spent together.

Of course, they made love, sometimes in the studio, sometimes in his bedroom if they made it that far, sometimes even out on the terrace. But to her surprise Leon hadn't only wanted to indulge in sex. He had taken her across to the

opposite hillside to show her the stunning site where Kaliq
had chosen to build his villa, and then for a drive along the
coast road with its magnificent cliff-top views. He had taken
her down to the harbour with its lively market, to the central
square with its endearing medieval church, and of course he
had brought her out here to the ocean.

And Montéz had unquestionably captured her heart,
Cally admitted, ignoring the nagging voice in her head
which said *and that's not the only thing*. But, whilst she
could get away with claiming that it was the natural beauty
of the island which was responsible for inspiring her to
work on her own painting whenever she got a spare
moment, she couldn't deny that ceasing to fight her sexual
appetite was responsible for the return of her much-missed
focus on the restorations. In fact, she had made so much
progress that after—how many weeks, three?—it wouldn't
be many more days before they were completely finished.

But it wasn't until she'd spotted a missed call on her
mobile and listened to the answer-phone message that
morning that Cally had really faced facts and realised that
she ought to start thinking about what she was going to do
next—which went for her relationship with Leon too. The
prospect shouldn't have felt like trying to remove a limpet
from the bottom of his boat—after all, that night in his
bedroom she had been heartened by the thought that their
lovemaking would reach an enforced conclusion rather
than waiting for his desire for her to wear thin—but it did.

Which was probably because in so many ways it didn't
feel just like lovemaking anymore. For, even though she
had resigned herself to the knowledge that theirs was a
passion that was destined to go nowhere, in these past few
weeks Leon had really opened up to her of his own accord.

He'd talked to her about his daily work at the university as they shared their evening meal; he'd told her about his time in the Marine Nationale. In turn she'd told him about her family and her degree, and they'd spent hours conversing about art, a subject upon which he had a knowledge more extensive than she would ever have imagined.

In fact, it felt pretty much like a real relationship in every way—except that their relationship was the one thing they didn't discuss, she thought, looking across at his beautiful body sprawled out beside her, his tanned chest glistening in the sunshine. Was it because, as far as he was concerned, it was already decided that the second she put down her paintbrush she'd be picking up her bags and leaving on the first plane home? He had told her himself that romance was in a Frenchman's blood, so perhaps this sex with added sentiment was just what you got with him, she thought dismally. Or was there a possibility that the reason he hadn't brought it up was because he didn't want her to go?

Not that it would change anything, even if he didn't, Cally quickly rationalised, because her career was what mattered first and foremost. So why did the answer-phone message, which ought to have had her jumping for joy, make her feel like she had been rudely awoken from the perfect dream?

'You know, I reckon it won't be much longer before my restorations are complete,' Cally said, trying to make her voice sound as blithe as possible.

Her words interrupted Leon's unruly thoughts. Thoughts which involved him rolling over and peeling down her black bikini top, which in his opinion had been on for far too long this afternoon, particularly now that the wet Lycra was beginning to dry in the coolness of the breeze and he could see the tight buds of her nipples that cried out for his mouth. Although on second thoughts it wasn't so much her words that had made that image vanish from his mind as her tone, which sounded offhand, as if the actual words were nothing but a code she expected him to crack. It was a tone he had never heard Cally use before, but ever since he had witnessed the starry look in her eyes that night Kaliq and Tamara had mentioned their forthcoming nuptials, ever since she had filled him in on her sparse sexual history, he had always feared she was in danger of adopting it. Had known too, that there was no way he was going to allow it to get to him, any more than he had any intention of allowing their lovemaking to come to an end. Yet.

'It hadn't escaped my notice.'

Cally rolled over, leaning on one elbow. 'So, will you be glad when I'm all done?'

His eyes remained closed. 'Of course. I cannot wait to see them both restored to their original glory.'

Cally hesitated. 'Me too. But I have to admit I shall be a little sad not to be working on them anymore, in that studio and—'

'Are you by any chance trying to induce me to ask you to stay on after you have finished, Cally?' Leon opened his eyes and challenged her with his piercing blue gaze. 'Because if you are may I remind you that *you* were the one who insisted that our lovemaking should only last whilst— how was it you delicately put it?—whilst your work on the Rénards placed us in close proximity to one another.'

Cally flushed, the previously pleasant heat of the sun now making her skin prickle uncomfortably. 'No, I— It just occurred to me this morning that I had finished them a little more quickly than I expected, that's all.'

'It's been a month, as you estimated.'

'A month?' Cally stared at him, dumbfounded. 'No, it can't have been.'

'Time flies when you're having fun,' he drawled, sitting up and drying his legs with a towel.

A month? A month in which they had made love pretty much every day, she thought, suddenly realising she hadn't had a period since before she had arrived. The heightened colour drained from Cally's face as she fished around in her mind for an explanation to quash her fears of the un-thinkable. Her periods were sometimes irregular, weren't they? And if anything was going to change a woman's cycle it was a different diet, a different climate from usual, wasn't it? Yes, that had to be it. In a couple more days, it was bound to arrive.

'Well, anyway, all I'm trying to say is that I hadn't given much thought to any future projects until I received a phone call from the Galerie de Ville in Paris this morning. They have just purchased a collection of pre-Raphaelite pieces and they are looking for an additional restorer to work with their existing team. The London City Gallery recom-mended me, and they want to meet to discuss whether I'd be interested.'

'Congratulations,' Leon replied gruffly. 'You should have said earlier. When's the meeting?'

'I don't know yet. As soon as possible, I think. I missed their call yesterday afternoon and I only picked up their answer-phone message this morning.'

'And you haven't called them back yet?'

'Not yet, no.'

Leon's momentary surprise evaporated. 'And why would that be, *chérie?* Because you wanted to ask me whether I thought it a golden career opportunity first? Surely not, for we both know that it is. Therefore you must be wavering because you wish to see whether I will offer you a more attractive alternative, *oui?*'

Cally flew to her feet. 'As if!' she shot out, terrified that was why she had wavered, that she had been willing to jeopardise her career for the sake of a man who felt nothing for her for the second time in her life. 'I suppose I just hoped you might show a little regret that our *affair* is inevitably reaching its end.'

'Inevitably? Why? Montéz is only ninety minutes away from Paris. You will have weekends, will you not?'

Cally's mouth dropped open. 'You mean... You wish it to continue?'

'Just because I do not ever wish to marry does not mean that I am not interested in extending a mutually pleasurable affair.'

He made it sound like their relationship was a library book he wanted to take out on six-week loan instead of three. Yet, wouldn't he end this now if she meant absolutely nothing to him? *Oh, don't be ridiculous, Cally. He'll end it eventually, so what's the difference?* Agreeing to let it continue could only prolong the hurt until the day he decided that he no longer found her satisfying. Which surely, if they were only to see each other at weekends, would be sooner rather than later for a man with a sexual appetite as insatiable as his. Unless, of course, exclusivity was not part of his offer in the first place, she thought with a start, feeling suddenly nauseous.

'And who will you make love to Monday to Friday, Leon?'

Leon's mouth twisted in disgust. 'You have my word that you will be the only woman sharing my bed.'

She stared at him, wanting to believe him, wanting to believe that it was possible to have a relationship and the career she loved, wondering if she even dared try. 'But why?'

Leon ran his eyes over her face. Her pale skin was flecked with light freckles brought out by the sunshine, the faint mark from her snorkelling mask was still visible on the bridge of her nose and her red hair was matted with seawater. It would have been easy to think to himself that her vulnerability was the reason, that she didn't deserve to be let down for the second time in her life, but the truth was that he had quite simply never seen anything so alluring and he didn't *want* her to go. Was it because she was the first woman who had come out on his boat like this? he wondered, trawling his mind for a logical explanation. No, there had been others, he recalled, surprised to find that his ex-lovers all blended into one faceless, nameless and frankly dull mass. But they had either demanded that he sail them across to St Tropez for lunch at a restaurant followed by an afternoon in the boutiques, or after a few minutes in the water had spent two hours below deck re-trowelling their make-up and ironing their hair. Yes, it had to be because he had never met anyone quite so appealingly *uninhibited* as she was.

'Because I've never wanted anyone as much as I want you,' he breathed, sensing her capitulation as he reached out his arm and dragged her towards him. 'And I'm not ready for this to end.'

Neither was she, she thought, forgetting all the reasons why this was a bad idea when he looked at her like that. And maybe, just maybe, if they both learned to trust, neither one of them ever would be.

'Then I hope you are not prone to dizziness, Leon,' she whispered.

'And why is that?'

'Because the first thing I want you to show me when you come and visit me in Paris is the Eiffel Tower.'

Leon paused. 'Maybe the second thing, *chérie*,' he said with a wicked gleam in his eye, before lowering his head to plunder her mouth.

Cally completed the restoration of the Rénards at lunchtime three days later. Standing back to admire them, she was overcome with a feeling quite unlike any other she'd experienced in her life. It always gave her a thrill to see a work of art restored exactly the way an artist had intended, but this transcended that; it was almost as if a part of her own personal destiny had been fulfilled.

She couldn't wait to show Leon. She looked at her watch. Twelve-thirty. He'd be back at two if not before. Which meant for the first time since that afternoon on the boat she had an hour alone to spare. Since there was still no sign of her period, she decided she really ought to take herself off to the pharmacy she'd spotted in the nearby village just to be sure it was just late and nothing more. That way, when she went to Paris to speak to the gallery tomorrow, at least she could go without any niggling concerns.

Unless of course the niggling concern turned out to be a full-blown worry-fest, she thought. She was still convinced she couldn't be pregnant when she felt absolutely no different from normal, aside from a little tiredness, which was probably due to the amount of time she spent making love to Leon or swimming in the sea. But what if she was? A slow and thoroughly unexpected warmth crept through Cally's body. She didn't know whether it was her buoyant mood or too much sun, but for some reason it didn't feel like something that would be a worry at all; it felt like it would be the most natural thing in the world.

Hearing footsteps approaching the studio door made a wide smile break out on her face. He was back early.

'Finished,' she said triumphantly. 'What *am* I going to do— Oh.'

Cally stopped mid-sentence as she turned round to discover the footsteps were not Leon's. On second thoughts she wasn't surprised, for she so rarely heard him enter, a trait she had come to associate with his natural diver's stealth. The feet belonging to the person who had entered, on the other hand, could not have been less subtle, for they were clad in bright-purple stilettos.

Cally took in the matching purple dress and blue-black hair which reached the woman's waist. A waist which she was sure would have ordinarily been no wider than the span of two hands, if she hadn't looked about five months pregnant.

'Can I help you?' Cally asked, raising her eyes to look at her face for the first time. Suddenly she realised that the woman she was looking at was Toria. Toria, whose face she recognised from the wedding photo that had graced every magazine cover the year she had married Girard. Toria, who, if Leon was to be believed, was nothing but bad news for a list of reasons as long as her hair. But he hadn't mentioned that she was expecting.

'I'm looking for Leo,' she purred, a look of disdain on her wide, painted mouth.

Cally flinched. 'You must be Toria.'

'And you must be his latest conquest.' Toria ran her eyes critically over Cally's paint-splattered outfit. 'How… charitable of him. Now, where is he, out *there?*' She motioned towards the sea in disgust.

'He's not here at the moment. Actually, I'm alone, and I rather thought all the doors were locked. Do you mind me asking how you got in?'

'Keys,' she said, reaching into her oversized designer handbag and producing a bunch full. 'Don't look so surprised. This *is* my home. Or, should I say, *was.*

Cally gritted her teeth. 'He's at the university. I have no idea what time he'll be back,' she lied, hoping to make her leave. She had no idea why Toria still had a set of keys, but Leon had said she only ever came back to Montéz to stir up trouble.

'Then I suggest you call him and tell him that I am here with some very important news.'

Cally was tempted to tell her what she could do with her suggestion, but she spotted the opportunity to forewarn Leon that she was here.

'Of course,' Cally replied with artificial sweetness. 'Do take a seat.'

Cally went into his office and dialled his mobile. It rang and rang but there was no answer. Skimming her eyes down a list of numbers on his desk, she found one for the principal's office at the university and tried that instead.

'*Bonjour.*'

Cally hesitated at the sound of the unfamiliar, accented voice. 'Um… *Je voudrais parler à Monsieur Montallier, s'il vous plaît.*'

The man on the other end of the phone clearly recognised her less-than-fluent grasp of French. 'This is Professeur Lefevre. The prince is not here, I am afraid. Can I help?'

'He has already left to return to the palace?' Cally asked hopefully.

'*Non, mademoiselle.* He has not been here today.'

'Oh.' Cally frowned, certain that he had told her he was expected there for the duration of the morning. 'So you haven't seen him at all since yesterday?'

'*Non,* you must be mistaken. I haven't seen him for at least…' Professeur Lefevre gave a considered pause. 'It must be three weeks at least.'

Her breath caught in her throat. 'Then I…I suppose I must have been mistaken. I'm sorry to have disturbed you.'

Cally continued to clutch on to the receiver long after he had hung up, her knuckles white. Leon had told her he had been at the university almost every day for the past month, but he hadn't been. She tried to tell herself it was no big deal. It was probably easier to say he was there than to go into details about his duties. But it grated on her. And now the woman he professed to hate had turned up with her own set of keys to the palace. She took a deep breath, trying to compose herself, remembering that their relationship was never likely to work if she was always so quick to distrust him. Plastering on a smile, she re-entered the studio.

'Men do have a warped idea of beauty,' Toria said, regarding the Rénards with a pinched look as Cally entered.

'Don't they,' Cally replied, looking right at her. 'I'm afraid Leon is otherwise engaged. For all I know, he could be hours.'

'Well,' Toria replied irritably, 'then I suggest, since I cannot be expected to wait around in *my* condition, that you give him a message.'

'Gladly.'

'Tell him I'm pregnant. With the heir to the throne.'

CHAPTER ELEVEN

CALLY stared at Toria aghast, dropping her eyes to the swell of her belly.

Pregnant. *With the heir to the throne.*

Her mind raced as she fought to process the information in some way other than a way which felt like a bullet tearing through her flesh. Toria had to mean that Girard was somehow the father, didn't she? But he had died a year ago, so that was impossible—unless via frozen sperm or IVF? No, she thought, his death had been too unexpected for that.

Cally lifted her eyes to the other woman's face, recalling how Leon had described her as 'incredibly attractive', how she had swung her own set of palace keys from her forefinger, purring his name. Suddenly Cally felt sick.

'Surely you don't mean that Leon…?' Her voice was scratchy, desperate.

Toria hesitated for a moment and then looked at her squarely. 'Yes. Leon is the father.'

Cally blanched and stumbled the short distance to the sofa, her whole body beginning to tremble. 'No. How?'

The other woman gave an acidic laugh. 'How? Surely I do not need to explain that to *you?* Leon Montallier is not an easy man to resist.' She shrugged. 'I made the mistake of believing that because I was his brother's widow he wouldn't set his sights on me unless his intentions were honourable. I was wrong.'

She paused for a moment, and then, seeing that Cally's head was safely buried in her hands, continued unreservedly. 'Afterwards I was so angry that I tried to go to the press, but he got there first. Thanks to his carefully engineered law, his pristine reputation on this island remains intact, just the way he planned it.'

Cally raised her head in horror.

'Oh, don't tell me, he spun *you* that line about reinstating the law to get on with his royal duties without the media circus as well?' Toria clicked her tongue scornfully. 'That was what the last one fell for. If I were you, I'd leave before he knocks you up and throws you out too.'

Cally closed her eyes, missing the malicious smile on the other woman's face.

'I'll bear that in mind,' she choked.

'Good,' Toria said, tossing her dark mane over her shoulder. 'And I trust you'll remember to give him my news. I'll see myself out.'

Cally gazed helplessly at a knot on the wooden floor of the studio. More than anything she had ever wanted in her life, she wanted to believe Toria was lying. She tried to think of her as the witch Leon had made her out to be, of her capacity for deceit. But the more minutes that ticked by the harder that seemed. She recalled the girl she'd worked with at David's father's estate, the one who had warned her about what he was really like, but who she had chosen to ignore. She couldn't help thinking that history was repeating itself—and that she really ought to have learned her lesson.

If Toria and Leon had been living here together after Girard's death, it hardly required a stretch of the imagination to envisage them falling into bed. And if he had romanced Toria the way he had romanced her, particularly under the delicate circumstances, it was no wonder that Toria had mistakenly assumed his intentions were honourable. Most of all it was remarkably easy to imagine his lust turning to disgust the second she'd attempted to sell her story. Cally had witnessed his anger when it came to the press herself.

And, though she knew Toria had taken a warped pleasure in telling her, even that only served to make her story seem all the more plausible. For she had exhibited exactly the kind of behaviour one might expect of a woman returning to an ex-lover with the news that she was carrying his child only to find another woman in her place.

Which could so easily have been her. Cally squeezed her eyes tightly shut, trying not to contemplate the unspeakable possibility that brought to mind.

What if they were both carrying his baby?

She felt the speed of her breathing double, the red of the sofa on which she sat and the blue of the sea outside the window starting to blur before her eyes as though she was spinning around on some garish purple fairground ride. She lay back, curling herself into a ball, threading her fingers through her hair to clutch at her skull, trying to block out everything.

But just as she was about to slip into the oblivion of unconsciousness she heard his voice.

'No wonder you're exhausted.'

It was soft and unbearably tender. Cally blinked and forced her eyes open. He was standing before the paintings, examining the final and most intricate part of her restoration with delight.

'It looks fabulous.'

She didn't move. 'I'm not exhausted.'

'No?' he queried, his eyes never leaving the canvas. 'In that case, how do you feel about celeb—?' He turned round and caught sight of her properly for the first time. 'What on earth's the matter?'

Cally pushed herself up on one arm, the blood rushing to her head. 'Toria was here.'

He visibly stiffened. *'Toria?'*

She nodded.

Leon looked incensed. 'What did she want?'

Cally took a deep breath. She was aware that she should probably tell him to take a seat, do this slowly. Aware, too, that it should never have been her news to tell. But above all, selfish though it was, she just wanted to get it out so that she could see his reaction—because she knew that alone would tell her everything she needed to know.

'She came to tell you that she's pregnant with your child.'

To her disbelief, he laughed. 'She has resorted to lies before to try and scare away any woman she sees as a threat, but this takes it to a whole new level. After everything I told you, I thought you'd know better than to believe a single word that comes out of her mouth.'

'It wasn't her words that convinced me,' Cally whispered brokenly. 'It was her sizeable bump.'

When she saw the look that came over Leon's face then, she would have given anything to have his cynical humour back. The blood shrank from his cheeks and his expression grew so taut that it looked as if his skin had been removed and stretched in order to cover the bones of his face. For the first time since they had met, she witnessed every last glimmer of sardonic amusement vanish from his eyes until there was nothing there but emptiness. It was the look which confirmed that everything she'd feared was true, and which banished Cally's last remaining shred of hope.

And that was the moment Cally knew that, if she had even one ounce of self-respect, she had to leave now. If nothing else, the entire stance of his body told her that the prospect of being a father was on a par to him with being told he had some horrible, degenerative disease. With it she understood that whatever she had started to believe about him opening up to her, human commitment of any form would always be unpalatable to him. She had to make sure *she* was not in danger of carrying his baby, and then she had to get on that plane to Paris and forget she had ever made love with the Prince of Montéz.

Slowly, on legs which felt like their muscles had disintegrated, she found the strength to stand.

'Where are you going?'

So she wasn't completely invisible. 'To Paris.'

'Your flight doesn't leave until tomorrow.'

She stared at him aghast. Surely he didn't actually expect her to stay? 'Under the circumstances, I hardly think—'

'Oh, but of course,' he said, snapping out of his temporary trance. 'Just because *she* says I'm the father, it *must* be true.'

So now that the initial shock had passed he had decided it was in his interests to deny it, Cally thought bitterly. She shook her head. 'Why would she lie?'

'Because she's a bitch, Cally, a cold-hearted, evil bitch.'

'So after Girard's death, when you were both living here, you're telling me you never went near her?'

Leon's mouth soured as if he resented having to explain himself to her. 'No, *I* never went near *her*.'

'What does that mean?'

'It means she lost no time in attempting to seduce me. What she wanted above all else was to be the wife of a prince, regardless of who the prince was. But I made it perfectly clear to her that I would rather stick pins in my eyes than go anywhere near her, and informed her of my intention to reintroduce the law against the press. She left the island almost immediately.'

'You never mentioned that when you told me about her.'

Leon shrugged. 'Compared to the rest of her sins, it's nothing.'

'So how come she still has keys to the palace?'

'Unfortunately for me, as she's Girard's widow there are some rights to which she is still entitled. Access to the palace is one of them.'

Cally closed her eyes, breathing deeply, feeling like she had been presented with the prosecution and defence in a trial for which she would face the punishment however she judged it, wishing she could be handed a simple picture which depicted the truth.

'Toria tells it very differently.'

'So you choose to believe her word over mine?' he bellowed incredulously. 'Why? Because the first time we met I neglected to mention my title? I thought we were past that.'

'We were.' Cally felt tears begin to prick behind her eyes and swallowed hard. 'That's why as soon as she arrived I tried to warn you by calling the university. But you weren't there, were you? You haven't been there for weeks, and yet you've been telling me you have!'

'I—'

'No. Let me finish. I told myself there had to be some logical explanation for that, and then I tried as hard as I could to believe that Toria wasn't telling the truth. That's why I waited to hear your side of the story. But that look of utter horror on your face when I told you she was pregnant told me everything I needed to know.'

Leon paused, and for a moment he actually contemplated telling her, but the thought of saying the words aloud was so agonising that he crossed his arms and turned away. 'I'm just horrified by the prospect of that witch bringing a child into this world.'

'How gallant of you to be so concerned about the life of an unborn baby.'

'It's an insult to the memory of my brother.'

'The merry widow doesn't fit into one of your neat little boxes for characterising women?' she shot out sarcastically.

'Like the giant box labelled "liar" that you have reserved for all men?'

'So, what, you're telling me that you were at the university all along?'

Leon scowled, wondering how the hell the one woman he had broken his rule for wasn't even capable of trusting him in return. 'Yes. Not at the main campus, but at another building off-site.'

'So why did the principal of the university know nothing about it?'

'Because I haven't shown it to him yet.'

Cally looked at him disbelievingly. 'So, show *me*.'

It was then that the room went ominously silent and Leon looked down at her with an expression that was even more crushing than the one she had read there when she had announced Toria's pregnancy. It was a withering look which told her she had just made the unforgivable mistake of assuming that he had to prove anything to her. And with it she saw with agonising lucidity that it really made little difference whether he was telling the truth or not, because she didn't mean anything to him, and she never would.

'And what if I did show you, Cally? Would you demand Toria has a paternity test before we can continue with our affair? Because we could, but something tells me even that wouldn't be enough. You were envious, were you not, when you met Kaliq and Tamara, so newly engaged? And now Toria claims to be having my child and you are practically inconsolable. Are you sure that you aren't so upset because what you *really* want is for me to propose we get married and start making babies of our own?'

Cally tried her best to steady her breathing as the colours of the room threatened to blur before her eyes again. 'No, Leon, what I want is to leave. I want to get on the plane to Paris, and I want to get on with my career.'

'Like hell you do, Cally Greenway.' He raked his eyes mercilessly over her body sending a renewed yearning hurtling through her bloodstream. 'Why cut off your nose to spite your face?'

Because if I don't stem my desire I'll lose my heart, Cally thought. 'Whatever is between us is over.'

'Over?' Leon laughed a low, impertinent laugh that seemed to reverberate around the whole room. 'This thing will never be over between us, *chérie.* It's too damned hot.'

She should have been quicker, but Leon was one step ahead, catching the top of her arm with his fingers and spinning her round easily to plant his lips on hers. His kiss was a kiss of possession, hot, furious and undeniably physical; it felt like he had poured his whole body into it, though only their lips were touching. She knew what he was doing as her treacherous body responded with predictable arousal thrumming through her veins, her nipples hard, longing for the press of his chest. Oh yes, he was waiting for her to succumb to him, to draw herself to him and clasp her arms around his back with all the wild abandon which she always did.

Not anymore. Abandoning her senses had got her into this mess, and it certainly wasn't going to get her out of it. She needed to escape now, while she at least had the promise of the career she had worked so hard for. Even if it seemed to have lost all its meaning.

But it had more meaning than his kiss ever would, a voice inside her cried, and somehow it gave her the strength to push herself away from him and she stumbled backwards, desperate to put as much distance between them as possible.

'Like I said,' he breathed, his chest rising and falling in double-quick time, his lips as swollen as hers felt. 'Too damned hot.'

No, she thought desolately as she drank in the sight of him against the backdrop of the ocean for one final time, *too damned cold.*

CHAPTER TWELVE

Four months later

CALLY wanted to like Paris. There were plenty of reasons why she should. For a start, professionally speaking, she could finally say that all the years of hard work and study had been worthwhile. The head of the conservation team at the Galerie de Ville had gladly employed her, and had done so based on her merits alone. The work was stimulating and the paintings prolific; last week they had showcased an early Rossetti that she and the rest of the team had restored, and it had been extremely well-received. The other conservationists were dedicated and friendly, the studio state-of-the-art. And, where once her lunch breaks had consisted of a dash down to the rather lacklustre local shops on the outskirts of Cambridge, now she could take a walk along the Seine, wander through the endless rooms of the Louvre, or, as had been her preference of late, sit in a café in Montmartre and watch the world go by.

When she was not at work, she returned to a small but pleasant apartment near the Eiffel Tower which she was renting from a dear old woman by the name of Marie-Ange who was also giving her French lessons, and with the help of Jen back home she had even arranged to get tenants into her house so that she wasn't out of pocket. What with her earnings from the Rénards, deposited in her account within a day of leaving Montéz, her bank balance looked positively healthy.

Oh yes, Cally thought, on the surface everything looked just dandy, that business with the Prince of Montéz far behind her. All except for a couple of minor details. Like the excruciating pain of finding herself in the most romantic city in the world with a broken heart. And the fact that she was pregnant with his baby.

Cally ran her hand protectively over her stomach as she looked across at the higgledy-piggledy rows of umbrellas and easels of the Place du Tertre and cast her mind back to the day she had left. She'd rushed into the pharmacy at Montéz airport as soon as Boyet had dropped her off, desperate to put her mind at rest before catching her flight. And then she had taken the test. Or rather she'd taken three tests, because each time she'd seen the positive result she had scuttled out of the toilet to buy another, convinced that the previous one had to be faulty. Until the sympathetic look of the pretty girl on the till had said it all, and she'd had to acknowledge that the evidence was irrefutable.

That was also the moment she'd realised that sympathetic looks were categorically not what she wanted. She might initially have been in denial about the possibility of being pregnant because of the less-than-perfect circumstances, but accepting that their lovemaking had created a new life growing inside her brought with it an innate joy that was as profound as it was unexpected. So much so that her first instinct had been to turn around and get a taxi straight back to the palace to share the magic of it with

Leon. But in her heart she had known that he would hate her for it. He'd probably have accused her of having planned it all along in some attempt to trap him into marriage, and then that look of utter horror would have come over his face the way it had when she'd told him about Toria. Toria, who for all Cally knew could be carrying her baby's older half-brother or half-sister.

That thought had had her running back to the airport toilets once more—this time with a violent nausea—and was what had convinced her to get on the first plane off the island. Of course, the most obvious final destination would have been England, and her nice, ordered life in Cambridge where she could have sat down and worked out how to go about this whole thing sensibly. But in a moment of hideous clarity she'd seen what would happen if that was what she did. Yes, she probably would have worked out a way to scrimp and save and continue with the bland restorations she'd survived on to date whilst raising a child. But then what? She would have grown into an old spinster, bitter that all those years of hard work and study had counted for nothing, that her only work of note was the Rénards, and that she'd only got to work on those because they happened to have been bought by a man who had wanted to bed her. And, worst of all, she would have remembered those weeks in Montéz as the highest point in her life because nothing in England was ever likely to eclipse them.

So, although it was the most unsuitable time to take a new job in an unfamiliar city, to Cally the possibility of a temporary contract with the Galerie de Ville offered her the chance to prove to herself that she had felt so alive on the island because of the creative challenge, the change of scene. Living in the French capital was bound to equal her experiences in Montéz, if not exceed them, and she would be placated by the knowledge that in years to come, as well as having achieved her dream of working as a restorer in one of the world's most prestigious galleries, she could look back on that time in her life much more rationally and be better prepared to face the challenges ahead.

But Cally had failed to take into account one very important variable.

Leon Montallier was not in Paris.

And, though she was loath to admit it as she dug into the delicious crêpe that the waiter had just placed in front of her, that was the reason she wasn't even close to the feeling of happiness she'd felt in Montéz. However perfect Paris was on paper, in reality it simply made her realise that everything she had always thought she wanted wasn't what she wanted at all. Even the new restorations which she was supposed to be enjoying were only vaguely satisfying in the sense that she was using her skills, filling her time. Creatively, the only thing she found herself wanting to do was create another composition of her own. But every time she sat down before a blank canvas she just couldn't bring herself to begin; it was as if the vast expanse of emptiness represented the contents of her heart.

It was probably for the best, she thought miserably. Yes, she'd thought that landscape she'd done at the palace had been all right at the time, but she was sure if she ever saw it again without the rose-tinted glasses of back then she'd know it was dire. She should have tossed it into the sea before she'd left, she thought, suddenly hideously embarrassed by the thought that by now Leon had doubtless come across it, vaguely recalled the conversation in which

she'd told him she never painted her own stuff and concluded there was a good reason why. He'd probably tossed
it into the sea himself.

And, as for supposing that once she was on her own the
gaping hole he'd opened would close again, she couldn't
have been more wrong. It was irrational, it was hopeless,
but the truth was she was in love with him, and there could
be no more denying it. Paris had only magnified the very
feelings for him which she had come here to try and dispel.
Feelings which, as the first few weeks went by, she had
hoped would be diminished by the passing of time, but
which remained stubbornly unchanged.

Unchanged, all except one thing. Last week she had been
practising her French translation by listening to a gossipy
radio station when suddenly she'd heard Toria's name.
Apparently she was celebrating the birth of her baby boy—
a beautiful, mixed-race baby boy—with her partner, a pro-
fessional footballer, with whom she was now living in Milan.

It was, of course, an enormous relief to Cally to know that
she wasn't in the running for some hideous Oprah Winfrey
show entitled *I'm pregnant with the prince's baby... Me too!*
But in some ways it made coming to terms with her own
actions even harder. For whatever reason—maybe purely to
stir up trouble for the man who had curbed her fame—Toria
had been the one spinning the lies, and Leon had been telling
the truth. Except about where he had been all those mornings,
she thought in a bid to continue to think ill of him, but now
that just seemed petty. That was hardly a crime—unlike not
telling someone they were going to become a parent.

Of course, she'd thought about it ever since. The instant
she'd heard the news on the radio she'd seriously toyed
with the idea of phoning him, or catching a flight out to

Montéz. But every time she imagined his response she lost her nerve. Discovering he was not the father of Toria's baby only changed things from her perspective, she thought as the waiter cleared her plate. Maybe she could trust him, but it didn't alter the fact that Leon did not want a child, and that if it hadn't been for her lust-induced idiocy Leon would not be having a child. So why should he have to feel some burden of responsibility to her and their baby for the rest of his life because of her mistake? She couldn't bear the thought of that. If he had wanted any further part in her life he would have come looking for her, but he hadn't.

'Mind if I join you?'

At the sound of a voice which sounded uncannily like his, Cally's head flew up so fast she saw spots and knocked her cup flying, the dregs of her coffee heading straight for him across the glossy red-and-white-checked tablecloth. She was just about to jump up and catch it, when he reached forward and stopped it with a napkin that he seemed to produce out of thin air and dropped into the chair opposite in one fluid movement.

'Leon.' Her voice came out altogether too breathlessly, part shock at seeing him here, part horror at the realisation that if she had jumped up, he would have seen the evidence of her pregnancy. 'What are you doing here?'

She shifted underneath the table, suddenly grateful for the cover it offered.

'One of your colleagues at the gallery told me I might find you here.'

'Who?' Cally asked, praying he'd spoken to Michel and not Céline, who was bound to have mentioned that Callie had been coming here every day since she'd developed a peculiar craving for spinach-and-gorgonzola crêpes.

'A man. I didn't catch his name.'

'Michel.' Cally smiled and breathed a temporary sigh of relief, not noticing the look of displeasure that flitted across Leon's mouth. 'Anyway, that wasn't what I meant. What are you doing here, in Paris?'

Her mind rewound to what she had been thinking about seconds before he'd appeared out of nowhere. *If he had wanted any further part in your life, he would have come looking for you...* Was it possible? She examined his face, the face that was etched so clearly in her mind that it was there even when she closed her eyes. It was even more devastating than she remembered, but, if it were possible, even more shuttered too.

'Why do you *think* I'm in Paris, *chérie?*' His look was depreciating, and for a second she was terrified he knew. No, he couldn't.

'You're here on business?' she ventured.

He chuckled, running his finger down the menu. 'Partly. What are you having?'

Partly. What the hell did that mean? It meant business and pleasure were always inseparable to him, she supposed, that maybe whenever his princely duties took him within a cab journey of an old flame he looked them up out of curiosity. Yes, Leon was the kind of man who would think it was possible to be friends afterwards, because he was never the one who got hurt. 'Nothing, thank you.'

'Then why don't you let me walk you back to the gallery?'

'Actually,' Cally backtracked, remembering the benefit of the table, 'I ought to have something or I'll be hungry later on.'

Leon gritted his teeth as she pretended to study the menu. The menu from which he had watched her order an enormous lunch less than twenty minutes earlier, and consume with a rapidity that would have made him think she wasn't earning enough money to feed herself properly if he hadn't known the truth. The truth that had stared him in the face from the newspaper article Boyet had left for his attention three days ago—the one about the new Rossetti the Galerie de Ville had on display, returned to its original glory by their team of restorers. With photographs.

At first he had been beside himself with fury. She was pregnant, and he knew the child had to be his—for he could accuse her of many things, but looseness was not one of them. Yet she had kept it from him, after all the accusations she had thrown at him about dishonesty and omitting the truth!

But, alongside his burning rage, he had realised that not only had she neglected to tell him, but she had not gone to the papers or come running back to him either. And that puzzled him. Yes, he had come to believe that maybe she wasn't the kind of woman who would sell her story for her fifteen minutes of fame as he had once believed, but he would have put money on her coming back to try and wangle a marriage proposal out of him. Hell, he had been convinced she would come back for the sex alone, just as soon as her desire for him threatened to consume her the way his desire for her had threatened to consume him so frequently in the weeks since her graceless departure, but to his infinite frustration she hadn't. So why hadn't she, even though she now had the perfect leverage?

The discovery that he did not have an answer to that question was the moment that it had occurred to him that, if he was capable of quelling his anger, then maybe, just maybe, she could be the perfect solution to the unpalatable problem which had been plaguing him ever since he'd heard about Toria. Along with the problem of the unbearable ache in his groin which had only increased at the sight of her newly voluptuous curves, he thought, observing her keenly through narrowed eyes and deciding it was time to find out if she really did suppose he was too stupid to notice.

'I think I'll have an almond *friand*,' Cally said, hoping it was the smallest thing on the menu. 'How about you?'

'I don't know. How about some answers?'

'Sorry?'

She tried to avoid his gaze but she felt his eyes bore into her. 'Some answers,' he repeated. 'Like why you haven't told me that you're having my baby.'

Cally felt a surge of panic knot itself around her heart. 'How—how did you find out?' she asked hopelessly.

'Not the way I deserved to.'

Her eyelids fluttered down to her cheeks and she nodded shamefully. 'I should have told you.'

'So why didn't you?'

She shook her head and fiddled with the menu, unable to look at him. 'Because I knew you didn't want a child, and it's my fault that you're having one.'

Leon frowned, not knowing what she meant, but certain he wasn't going to like what was coming next.

'That first time—when I said I didn't need protection— I thought we were talking figuratively. I didn't realise that... It wasn't until afterwards that I realised that you were talking about contraception.'

'So after that you just lived the lie, whilst accusing *me* of deceit at every opportunity?'

She hung her head.

Leon felt a white-hot anger blaze within him but he forced himself to bite his tongue. If she had come to him with that excuse he never would have believed her, he would have known that it was all part of an elaborate ploy to get him to waltz her down the aisle from the start. But she hadn't. The fact remained that she'd had the perfect reason to throw in her career and get everything he'd thought she wanted but she hadn't used it. Which was why, even though he was livid that she'd lied, it was almost possible that this could work.

'It was an easy mistake to make,' he forced out, biting his lip.

Cally raised her head in utter disbelief. Understanding. From Leon Montallier.

'Yes, it was.'

'And yet you planned to see the consequences through.'

'Just because it was unexpected does not mean I even thought for a moment about not having this baby,' she shot back, a fierce and thoroughly arousing maternal protective-ness glowing in her eyes.

'So what you are saying is since discovering you are to become a mother, your feelings towards the idea of becoming a parent have changed?'

'Yes.'

'Did it not occur to you that if you had told me I was to become a father my feelings might have altered also?'

Cally watched as the lines of his face softened and her eyes widened in disbelief. 'I—I suppose I expected you to react in the same way that you did when I told you that Toria was pregnant,' she said guiltily. 'But I know now that had nothing to do with you.'

Leon nodded gravely, determined not to invite questions

about the real reason for his horrified reaction that day, but Cally was too lost in her own thoughts to notice.

'So, have they changed?' she whispered. 'Your feelings, I mean?'

Leon paused, knowing his answer demanded the utmost consideration, and took a deep breath. 'You are right that I did not expressly want a child, Cally. Not because of any aversion to the prospect, but because I believe that a child is best brought up by a mother and father who are married. Since I have always been disinclined on that front, by default the prospect seemed unlikely. But life is never quite that—neat.' He shook his head and turned away the waiter who had approached the table. 'You *are* carrying my child.' He ran his eyes over her face, surprised to find that the words were ready on the tip of his tongue without any of the resistance he had expected. 'But, even before I knew that, for the past four months I have found myself aching for you in a way that is completely unprecedented—not only to have you back in my bed, but to have you by my side.'

The heavy lashes that shadowed her cheeks lifted in disbelief.

'I therefore find that my inclination has changed. I wish to marry you, Cally. As soon as possible.'

Cally had to pinch her leg under the table to check that she wasn't dreaming. Leon Montallier—*Prince* Leon Montallier, the man who had told her that he found the institution of matrimony categorically intolerable—hadn't *really* just said aloud that he wished to marry her, had he?

Yes, she thought. He had. And, impossible though it seemed, he'd said it in such a way that it sounded like the sincerest thing he'd ever uttered. It hadn't been some overblown, rehearsed proposal that befitted the romantic reputation of his countrymen; it had been a statement, simple and unadorned. It said that, no, this hadn't been the way he had expected things to go, but now that they had he wanted to take this chance because he felt what they had already shared could continue to grow. It said that he trusted her, and he was asking her to place her trust in him right back.

Could she? she wondered. Could she really dare to believe in things that she had spent years, and in particular the last four months, forbidding herself to even dream about? Like sleeping with the man she loved every night and waking up beside him every morning. Taking breakfast at the table on the terrace, a table laid for three, maybe one day even four. Cally closed her eyes to stop the visions overwhelming her. Surely those kinds of dreams were too big? Like he said, life wasn't neat. Even if they could tidy it now, what happened when the swell of unexpected feelings that had hit him with the discovery that he was to be a father diminished, and he remembered that he had never been cut out for family or fidelity after all? Wouldn't she be doing them both a wrong not to be more cautious?

'Don't you think that maybe getting married is a little too *rash?*' she replied hesitantly, focussing on the caricaturist and the small crowd of onlookers on the opposite side of the street, afraid that if she caught his eye he would know that talking him out of this was the last thing she really wanted.

'No,' he replied, his voice gentle but firm. 'And I'm not sure that you do either.'

Cally felt her breath catch in her throat, taken aback to discover that he didn't need to look in her eyes to know exactly what she was thinking. To know that she was looking for a reason to say no because it felt safer, because that was the answer that her nice, ordered life had got her into the habit of. And she understood that even if they'd been in a proper relationship for a year and had already had a conversation about what they'd call their children one day, saying yes would still feel just as scary because it involved her placing her trust in another human being. Rash was just an excuse.

'Perhaps you're right,' she admitted. 'But I just don't want either of us to look back and think this was a mistake.'

'No one can know what the future holds,' he said with all the gravity of a man who had experienced the arbitrariness of fate. 'But surely it could never be a mistake to try and raise our child together?'

He had her there, Cally thought, for how could she ever regret raising their baby with him in Montéz when the alternative was going it alone in her damp two-up two-down in Cambridge? However much she'd once hated the concept of privilege, she couldn't think of any better start in life for their child than growing up at the palace. Besides, she realised with a start, he or she would be first in line to the throne; how could they grow up anywhere else and be prepared for what lay ahead?

Leon hadn't even mentioned that, and suddenly she loved him all the more for it. Of course it would be important to him that his heir be raised on the island, yet he hadn't pushed it, just like he hadn't stressed that her acceptance would mean an official role for her too. But it would, she thought anxiously, wondering whether saying yes would mean kissing everything in her old life goodbye.

'As well as raising our child, I had hoped to continue working, Leon.'

'Of course,' he replied with none of the sarcasm she might once have expected. 'Perhaps you can freelance out of the studio.'

Cally almost couldn't believe her ears. He wasn't asking her to give up the work she loved, he wasn't assuming that that was what she wanted. Yes, there were so many unknowns, so much to overcome, but surely if they were both willing to try…? 'Perhaps I could.' She nodded tentatively.

'Are you by any chance thinking that you wouldn't be averse to the idea of marrying me either, *chérie?*'

'Yes, Leon, I think I am.'

'Good,' he said, leaning across the table and whispering in her ear. 'Because I've already booked the church for this time next week.'

'This time *next week?*'

Leon nodded.

It was arrogant. Maybe it was overly romantic too. But the joy in her heart overtook her exasperation and in an instant she was on her feet and closing the short distance between them. But just as she pressed her body into his and raised her hands to tangle them in his hair he placed one hand on her elbow and stopped her.

'What is it?'

Cally followed his eyes, which had dropped to her pregnant stomach.

'I just—' It was the first time it had really occurred to him that his child was growing inside her womb, and he was shocked by the feelings of both helplessness and strength that swelled within him. 'Can I touch it?'

'Of course you can!' Cally grinned, breathing a sigh of relief and grabbing his hand to place it on her belly. She was equally unprepared for the weight of her own emotions as he stroked her protectively.

'I'm sorry,' she whispered, drawing in a deep breath as the magnitude of what she had denied him truly hit home. As she did, her agitation caused the baby to give a tiny kick. He jumped back and looked at her in awe.

'I'm sorry I didn't tell you,' she repeated.

Leon felt a muscle tighten at his jaw but he forced himself to let it go.

'My twenty-week scan—it's booked in at the hospital here in three days. Come with me?'

He nodded with a conviction that told her he wouldn't miss it for the world. 'And then to Montéz.'

CHAPTER THIRTEEN

'How about Jacques?' Leon grinned as they drove over the hilltop and the palace came into view. It was even more resplendent than she remembered in the low November sunshine.

Cally looked down at her lap. She was holding their marriage licence which they had just collected from the town hall in one hand, and the ultrasound photo of their baby boy in the other. If she had had a third hand she would have pinched herself again.

'Inspired by Jacques Rénard?' she asked, studying the photo as only an expectant mother could, ignoring the fuzzy patches of light and shade and trying to discern whether their son might look like a Jacques. She turned back to Leon and her smile widened in approval. 'I love it.'

They had both wanted to know the sex. Maybe it was because having a baby in the first place had been surprise enough, or maybe it was because they had both wanted to discover one thing about this pregnancy together, but either way they were delighted.

'Remind me again of your nephews' names?'

'Dylan and Josh. Dylan's the eldest.'

It continued to amaze her that Leon had not only insisted

her family be invited to their wedding in four days' time, but that he seemed genuinely interested in them too—even Jen, despite her being a journalist, which she knew deep down he viewed as a heinous crime. However, Cally's amazement couldn't be greater than her sister's had been when she'd called her yesterday.

'Married? To the Prince of Montéz?' Jen had cried when she'd finally stopped apologising for the hundredth time for only hearing 'I wish' and 'Don't mention him' during that telephone conversation when she'd suggested running the article. 'But… I thought you said he was a complete bastard?'

'He has his moments.' Cally had laughed. 'But I've fallen in love with him, Jen, and, well… We're expecting a baby in March.'

Her sister had been even more flabbergasted then. But she decided that no one could be more amazed than she already was herself as she drew up outside the palace and she saw Boyet descending the steps, ready to unload the car of the few bits and pieces she'd brought with her to begin their new life together. Like the beautiful cot that had been a farewell gift from Michel, Céline and the rest of the gallery team, and enough knitted babygrows from Marie-Ange to clothe the entire maternity ward—she had been beside herself to discover that she had been renting a room to a future princess and heir of Montéz.

Yes, she would always recall the friends she had made in Paris with affection, but leaving the capital had been a million times easier than it had ever been to leave here, she thought as they walked through the courtyard and up the creamy white staircase. Montéz felt like home. And, whilst living in a palace was going to take some getting used to, she couldn't help believing her parents had actually been right when they had once told her that wealth and class could be irrelevant. She couldn't help hoping she'd been wrong to stop believing in happy-ever-after too.

Even if there had been a few moments in the past few days when the look in Leon's eyes had been so unfathomable it was like he had momentarily shut her out in the cold. But she told herself it was to be expected, that it was just going to take time for two people who weren't used to sharing their lives to learn to live with one another. She tried to repress the nagging fear that he'd always be closed to her, the realisation that he hadn't once asked how *she* actually felt about *him*. Was it because he didn't want to make her say things that he thought she might not be ready to say? Or because those things would never matter to him?

'*Bonjour, mademoiselle.*'

Cally shook herself and smiled warmly as Boyet opened the car door for her. '*Bonjour, Boyet, ça va?*'

'*Oui, ça va bien, merci.*' He grinned, clearly impressed with her improved accent, and then turned to Leon. 'I alighted upon a newspaper article that may be of some interest, Your Highness. The daily papers are out on the terrace as usual.'

He nodded '*Merci,* Boyet.'

Cally and Leon entered the hallway together, and whilst she popped to the bathroom Leon continued through to the terrace. He was standing above the wrought-iron table when she entered the drawing room, and she observed him as she walked towards the glass doors; his forehead was deeply lined.

'What is it?' she asked anxiously, stepping outside to join him. He raised his eyes casually from the article he was reading, but the second they met with hers he froze. For one long moment he seemed to look at her as if he was seeing her for the first time, and then his frown disappeared altogether and his whole face seemed to lighten.

'It's nothing, *chérie*,' he said, folding up the sheaf of paper and placing it in the top pocket of his shirt. 'Nothing at all. But I'm afraid there are some documents which urgently await my signature at the Treasury.' His eyes dropped to her hand that was still clutching their marriage licence and he smiled. 'I can drop our papers in with Father Maurice on the way. It's been a long day. Why don't you get some rest?'

Why don't you tell me what the article is about, if it's nothing? Cally wanted to retort, but she knew that she was probably just being paranoid, and making him aware of it was hardly going to encourage him to open up. 'You're probably right.'

Leon ran his finger tenderly down her arm and took the papers from her hand. 'I know I am.' He grinned. 'I'll be back in an hour or two, and if you're up to it we can take a stroll along the beach before dinner. It's not quite as warm at this time of year, but the sunset is always spectacular.'

She nodded as he kissed her lightly on the mouth. 'I'd like that.'

Cally tried to nap, but failed. Her mind was too full of all that had happened over the last few days and, if she was honest, too troubled by old insecurities. Which was ridiculous; she was lying on the royal bed, carrying his son, with their wedding just days away.

It was probably just coming back to the palace and trying to get her head around actually living here, she reasoned. For, though she had resided here for that month, it had been as nothing more than his lover and his employee, and as a result she hadn't really ventured beyond his bedroom or the studio. Cally sat up and swung her legs over the edge of the bed, feeling the luxurious rug beneath her toes. If she was to embrace her new life and feel comfortable raising their son here, then it shouldn't feel like the palace was just a sea of closed doors without any idea what lay behind them. *Like Leon,* she thought bleakly, and then scolded herself. It was going to take time. And, since he'd only just been saying that they should choose a room for the nursery, opening a few doors—literally—seemed like the perfect place to start.

Cally exited the master bedroom and turned right. There had to be at least eight other rooms she'd never entered just in this wing, never mind in all the other wings on the other floors. But she couldn't imagine choosing a room for their son's nursery—Jacques' nursery—more than a few steps away from their bedroom.

The first door she entered, opposite the master bedroom, revealed a large room with an oak ceiling and a view of the inner courtyard. It would have fulfilled its function more than adequately, but it didn't feel in any way cosy, and it seemed a shame to Cally for their son's room not to face out to sea when that was the part of Montéz that she most associated with Leon. The second room she entered was to the right of their own, and couldn't have been more different. It was a moderate size with a fabulous view of the bay, a long window seat and lemon walls bathed in late-afternoon sunlight. She could just imagine the cot in here. A rocking horse, piles of play bricks. She smiled, running one hand over her belly, and felt her heart settle. All it needed was some brightly coloured paintings, she thought, catching sight of a large frame propped face down against the wall and wondering if she could make use of it.

Cally walked towards it and wiped the dust from the edge of the frame with her finger. Leaning it back against her body to discern whether or not it was empty, she saw that behind the glass was an enormous royal-family tree. Fascinated, she carefully manoeuvred the frame so that it was propped against the wall face up and sank to her knees to survey it.

Leon so rarely spoke about his family. Not that she could blame him for that, for she had gathered that both his parents were dead and the pain of losing Girard was still very raw. But she couldn't help being curious about the royal dynasty that, incredibly, she found herself about to marry into, that her son was going to be a part of. She ran her eyes along row after row of unfamiliar names, sovereign princes past, their wives, their children. Then she dropped her eyes to the bottom of the picture, desperate to find Leon's name, to trace the branches she knew and to locate the spot where two new ones would soon be added. But the second she saw the swirling typescript of his name she dropped her hand as if she had been burned, shocked to discover that the existing branches around him didn't even begin to lead where she'd expected.

Rapidly, she tried to make sense of what she was seeing. Leon's mother Odette had married Arnaud Montallier, the Sovereign Prince of Montéz, and together they'd had one son—Girard. Seventeen years later, Girard was crowned Prince—the same year, quite logically, that his father had passed away. But it wasn't until the *following* year that Odette had given birth to her second son, Leon. Whose father was not listed as a prince at all, but as a man named Raoul Rénard.

Cally stared in disbelief. No wonder Leon had implied that his title was a fate that should never have befallen him. It was not simply because Girard had died unexpectedly, but because the royal bloodline—if it was like any other she'd ever read about—had technically died out with him. Which meant that Leon had inherited the throne simply because his mother had been the sovereign's widow.

Cally felt an icy fear begin to grip her as all that that meant slowly began to hit home. Her eyes rested on the branch between Girard and Toria. Toria, who was the former sovereign's widow just as Odette had once been. Toria, who had also given birth to a son. A son who—if Leon was an example of what happened in such circumstances—could inherit the throne one day. Unless Leon married and had a child of his own.

Suddenly, Toria's words that afternoon in the studio echoed through her mind with new and devastating clarity: *Tell him I'm pregnant. With the heir to the throne.* That was why the expression on Leon's face had been one of such unmitigated dread. She'd been so convinced she understood it, but she had actually read it as wrongly as she always did. It wasn't because he was the father of her child; oh no, Cally understood now that Toria had simply alighted on that lie as a way of hurting her. It was because the woman he loathed was carrying a child who had the potential to inherit everything.

And, with that realisation, the trust that Cally Greenway had dared to place in Leon Montallier came crashing down around her shoulders, taking her fragile heart with it. He hadn't come to Paris because he had missed her, hadn't proposed because he thought they had a shot at happiness, or even because he thought it was the best thing to do for their child. He had simply discovered that she was pregnant, and that making their child his legitimate heir was preferable to the thought of Toria's child being first in line to the throne. Hell, he'd even waited until he had accompanied her to the scan before they had gone to get their marriage licence. Fit, healthy and a boy; no wonder he'd proceeded with such enthusiasm!

Cally felt a tortured moan escape her lips and sank back on her heels, head raised as if appealing to some invisible god for mercy. Could she have been any more foolish? How easily she had fallen for his honeyed words and feigned understanding! She'd even supposed that he hadn't mentioned the small matter of their child's legitimacy because he didn't consider that to be the most important thing! Why the hell hadn't she learned that with Leon the important thing was always the thing that he *didn't* mention? Like the fact that he was a prince, that he had bought the paintings for himself, that he had only employed her because he wanted to take her to bed. He had lied to her from the day she had met him, and all this time she had been stupid enough to go on believing what she wanted to believe, thinking he simply needed time to open up.

Unable to bear the evidence of his lies in black and white before her, Cally backed away from the family tree and stumbled out into the corridor. Suddenly the whole palace felt like a conspirator in his betrayal. Tearing down the stairs and out into the grounds, she found herself on the grass verge overlooking the magnificent bay. The bay where Leon had planned to take her for a walk before dinner, that had been the subject of the picture he had inspired her to paint after so many years of believing that part of her was dead. Now every part of her felt dead, oblivious to everything except the sobs which began deep inside her chest and took her over. She couldn't remember the last time she had succumbed to such irrepressible tears, but she did know that her practised mechanism of swallowing hard and blinking repeatedly would do her no good, for her eyes were already sore, and her throat was so constricted it was all she could do not to choke on her own sobs.

She didn't even stop as she sensed him come up behind her. Looming. Blurred. She wanted to lunge at him, pound her fists against his chest, but she didn't have the strength.

He swooped down to her level. 'What the hell's the matter, are you in pain? The baby?'

'No, Leon,' she gasped, her words punctuated by sobs. 'The heir to the throne is perfectly safe.'

His brows descended into a dark V, and he ran his eyes over her as if checking all her limbs were intact. 'If not the baby, then what?'

'What else is there?' she swiped.

'Well, clearly there's something the matter with you, and I think I have a right to know.'

'A right to know?' Cally cried hysterically. 'You mean like I had a right to know that the only reason you wanted to marry me was because you couldn't bear a child of Toria's to be first in line to the throne?'

Leon went very still. 'Has she been here again?'

A ridiculous part of her had been waiting for him to deny it all. His response only drove the knife in deeper. 'No, Leon. Toria has not been here. Your pathetic little fiancée worked it all out by herself, from the family tree.'

Leon clenched his teeth. The family tree in his old nursery. The one his mother had given him as a child to try and help him come to terms with the truth, but which had only succeeded in making him feel more different.

'What were you doing, poking around in there?'

'Poking around?' she rasped despairingly. 'I thought this was to be my home, Leon, our son's home?'

'And so it will be.'

'No, Leon.' Cally shook her head. 'How can this ever become my home if there are parts of it I am forbidden to enter? Unless all you want is a wife in name only…' She looked out at the horizon, still trying to come to terms with her discovery. 'Yes. I suppose that *is* all you want.'

'I do not want you as my wife in name only!' he protested—too loudly, she thought, as he raised back up to his full height and began to pace.

'But unless you're prepared to be honest,' she whispered brokenly, 'how could I ever be anything else?'

Leon stilled, and, lowering his eyes, he caught sight of a single tear rolling down her cheek. As it splashed onto her pregnant belly, something unbearable began to invade every organ in his body. Shame? Regret? Fear? No, all three. That afternoon, when she'd left here for Paris, all he had wanted was her trust, to believe that her hysterics weren't some attempt to weasel something out of him. Now he realised that in agreeing to become his wife she had put her trust in him unquestionably, but he'd been so bloody single-minded—so driven by the solution she presented, by his own libido—that he'd trampled all over the one thing he had wanted to protect.

He dropped to the grass beside her, knowing it was too late, but that more than anything she deserved to know the truth, however shameful. 'How I became the prince isn't exactly something I'm proud of.'

Cally read the look of agony on his face. 'Well, you should be,' she said grudgingly. 'Whatever else is true, giving up a career you were passionate about because your country needed you is admirable.'

'It was my duty. It's complicated how that came to be the case, but it was.' He took a deep and ragged breath, his eyes fixed on the horizon. 'My mother's marriage to Arnaud was arranged by her social-climbing parents. It was an entirely loveless match, but she provided him with the son he desired and stayed loyal to him until he passed away. A few months after that, when she was still only in her late thirties, a sailor ran into trouble in the bay and she offered him shelter inside the palace whilst he repaired the engine on his boat. His name was Raoul Rénard.' Leon paused over his name, a tortured expression in his eyes, and suddenly its significance dawned on Cally. 'According to my mother, he was a descendent of the great artist Jacques Rénard. She fell deeply in love with him, and within weeks she was pregnant.'

Cally looked at him in wonder. That was why he had been willing to pay any sum for the paintings, and why he'd done so anonymously too: Jacques Rénard was one of his ancestors! She immediately felt guilty, for all the accusations she'd thrown at him about wanting them purely to boast about, and for how quickly she had jumped to the wrong conclusions about him. But they hadn't been all wrong, she thought, wiping the stream of tears from her eyes with the sleeve of her cardigan. Even if he did have a deep attachment to the paintings, he still had no real attachment to her. If he did, he would have told her sooner, would have understood that her own passion for the Rénards ran just as deep. And he would have proposed because he loved

her, she thought, stifling a renewed sob, not just because
he needed a son.

'And did he love her?' Cally asked, wondering why, in
spite of everything she had always known about true love
being the stuff of legend, not history, she wanted to hear
that he had.

'Yes.' Leon nodded gravely. 'I believe he did. But my
mother's moment of happiness was short-lived. The next
time my father returned to sea, the boat's engine caught fire
and he was killed.' His eyes clouded as he recalled that the
twist of fate which had been responsible for the start of his
life had also led to his father's death. 'The shock sent my
mother into labour early, and as a result the people of
Montéz simply presumed that Arnaud was my father. My
mother's closest advisors suggested that was for the best.
And, besides, I was the next in line regardless.'

Cally frowned. 'But...how?'

Leon replied in a voice that seemed to come from a long
way off, and Cally realised that the guard she had been
wanting him to drop ever since that night in London was
slowly coming down before her eyes. But only now did she
see that she had been wrong to assume that behind that
closed door would be the proof that he loved her; the reality
was that he felt nothing for her at all. Which probably
ought to have fuelled her anger, but all she could think
about was how much he'd had to deal with, how much she
wanted to hold him.

'The royal bloodline in Montéz differs from that of other
countries, or at least it has since the turn of the sixteenth
century,' Leon continued, watching the breeze blow wisps
of her hair out of her ponytail, wishing he had the right to
smooth them away from her face, hating that he didn't.

'At that time, the king of the island, who had subjected the islanders to a long reign of oppression, was overthrown by a hero amongst the people named Sébastien. He was the tyrannical king's illegitimate half brother—the son of the old king's widow and one of the palace advisors. Sébastien declared that the royal family should be abolished and that Montéz should become a democracy. The people were overjoyed, but they clamoured for him to become the king. He was reluctant, but eventually he agreed, on one condition: that he and his future successors should only ever be known as Sovereign Prince, not King, as a reminder that the greatest power should always remain with the people.'

At what point had he lost sight of what mattered? Leon wondered, and what made him even think that his son would be the worthiest successor to the throne with *him* as a role model? He shook his head and continued. 'But the rest of France was reluctant to accept Sébastien as the new sovereign, because he couldn't prove that he was royal. The citizens of Montéz were outraged, and so, to grant him legitimate status, they voted for a change to the law. It states that any widow of the sovereign retains her royal status after his death, and thus any child she bears afterwards inherits that status and a claim to the throne, so long as she never marries again. Therefore, they argued, Sébastien's mother had passed her royal status on to him.' Leon took a deep breath. 'As my mother did to me.'

Cally stared at him in amazement as all he had said sunk in, and the knock-on effects of the ancient and remarkable law began to crystallise in her mind. No wonder he had always spoken of his title as if it was something that didn't really belong to him, but a job that he had reluctantly taken on. And no wonder he had always found the concept of marriage so intolerable. For when the sovereign of Montéz took a bride, he had to trust her to honour him not only during his lifetime but even after his death.

Which meant he had been willing to place that trust in you, a voice inside her whispered, but she ignored it, for what good was that if she couldn't trust *him?* And what good had it done her to think this was just about feelings like trust or love, when he was a prince for whom marriage and children would always mean something more? Or was it really something less? she wondered sorrowfully.

'So, there you have it,' Leon concluded uneasily. 'I am the prince, but only because of an ancient technicality. In terms of the usual rules of patrilineal descent, I do not have a drop of royal blood.'

Cally's heart filled with empathy. 'Do you really suppose it matters whose blood runs through your veins, Leon?' she answered croakily, conscious that not so long ago she had been guilty of pigeonholing anyone with a title. 'Why should it matter who your father was, whether you inherited the throne because of a technicality or because of biology? What matters is that the prince has the best interests of his country at heart. That was why the people supported Sébastien all those years ago, the same way your people would support you.'

'Perhaps.' Leon turned back to her, his eyes searching her face in wonder, wishing he hadn't allowed the shame he felt for a past over which he had no control jeopardise his future with the only woman he had ever met who hadn't cared who he was, who had cared only whether he was a decent man. Well, he thought grimly, he had proved that he wasn't that all by himself. 'Not long after Girard passed away, the truth began to gnaw at me so badly that I almost made up my mind to find out. But I rcaliscd it would not only cause enormous unrest during an already turbulent time, but it would become common knowledge that any man who got Toria pregnant would be the father of the next Prince of Montéz, the consequences of which could have been catastrophic.'

'But Toria herself has always known?' Cally replied, her mind returning to the agonising present.

'Girard explained the intricacies of the law when they married, but it wasn't until after his death that she saw the opportunity to use what she had once seen as some boring old decree to benefit herself. When I resisted her advances, she realised that if she went to the papers with it it would ensure her a permanent following. That was what finally convinced me to reinstate the law against the press.'

'So the only way left for her to take revenge on you was by actually getting pregnant?' Cally stared agog, horrified that any woman could possibly use their potential for motherhood in such a despicable way.

'At the time I thought so, but now I believe that angering me, attempting to drive a wedge between you and me, was a convenient by-product of an accidental pregnancy.'

'Just like the solution to that problem was a convenient by-product of mine,' Cally said despondently, tugging on a piece of grass.

'I can't pretend that isn't partly true.' Leon's eyes were hooded, self-condemning. 'But it isn't that simple. I was always adamant that I never wanted to marry.'

She could understand that now, Cally thought, if not because of the peculiarities of the law then because of the loveless marriage his mother had endured, the union of misplaced trust his brother had fallen into.

He continued. 'I've always been adamant that I didn't want to marry, but once I met you I had to keep inventing new reasons why that was the case, because you kept proving all the old ones wrong. Like thinking all you wanted was fame or sex. By the time you went to Paris there weren't any reasons left.'

'Even if that is true—' Cally shook her head '—you still didn't do anything about it until you discovered that it was in the interests of your kingdom to act. And maybe I would have understood that too if you'd told me. But you didn't.'

Leon nodded remorsefully. 'I suppose I was still reluctant to admit it to myself, too scared you'd walk away if you knew and... And then it stopped having anything to do with my kingdom anyway.'

'What?' Cally searched his face as he reached into his pocket and unfolded the newspaper article he had put there that morning, the one he had refused to show her, and placed it down on the grass.

At the centre was a wedding photo, Toria's wedding photo, taken yesterday. Cally ran her eyes over the frothy white dress, the groom's garish white suit and their baby son dressed like a cherub as she tried to process what it meant. Leon's words rang through her mind: *Any widow of the sovereign retains her royal status after his death, and thus any child she bears afterwards inherits that status and a claim to the throne,* so long as she never marries again...

What it meant was that the second that Toria had got her figure back marrying a high-profile footballer had appealed to her more than revenge. It meant that Toria's son was no longer in line to the throne. And that meant, as of a few hours ago, Leon had had every reason to call their wedding off.

But he hadn't, because he'd taken their marriage

licences to the priest after that. She looked up into his face, her eyes enormous. 'You mean you don't *need* to marry me, but you were going to anyway?'

CHAPTER FOURTEEN

LEON nodded slowly, and part of Cally's heart felt like it was about to explode with unmitigated joy.

He doesn't need to, but he wants to marry you anyway, she repeated to herself.

Yet the other portion of her heart knew that whatever his reasons for wanting her to be his wife now, love couldn't possibly be one of them. If he had loved her, he would have told her the truth about his past months ago, or a week ago, or even this morning. He would have wanted to be open with her and to find out how she felt about him. But he hadn't, and he'd only told her now because she had accidentally stumbled upon his family tree.

'I understand why you were reluctant to tell me,' she said hopelessly. 'I even admire the whole host of practical reasons you had for proposing. But when I agreed to marry *you*...' She shook her head, knowing that now was the time for honesty on her part too, however futile. 'It was because I was in love with you. I think I was from the first moment I laid eyes on you in London, and because of that I thought I could marry you even if you never loved me. But I can't.'

As Leon listened, he felt something deep within him

shift. Once he'd believed that women only used words like 'love' as a means to an end, but Cally meant everything and wanted nothing. And that was the blinding moment when he realised that her love was everything he wanted, but the last thing that he deserved. Which was why, though the three little words hovered on his lips to say right back, he knew they weren't enough.

He took a deep breath, wondering if he was capable of even half her integrity. 'Let me show you something.'

'What?'

'Let me show you something.' Leon rose to his feet, tentatively reaching out his hand to lead her somewhere—to the car parked on the driveway, by the looks of things—but not daring to touch her. He was probably afraid her emotion was contagious. So, the *L* word really did mean nothing to him, she thought. Was he just going to pretend she hadn't mentioned it at all?

'Now?' she asked disbelievingly.

'Yes, now.' His brows creased with concern as he eyed her bump. 'If you can.'

Cally was too emotionally exhausted to argue. So she let him help her into the passenger seat of the car. The plain and perfectly ordinary black car, she noticed dismally as he pulled away, wishing it could have been some ridiculous sports model so that she could loathe its excess. That would have been easier. Easier than thinking about the real reason he had spent a fortune on those paintings, or why he had always been happiest out in the ocean. Things that reminded her that he was not just a billionaire prince with an overly complex family tree, but a man, a man who she admired more than she'd ever thought possible.

Eventually, after what felt like an age of twisting and

turning along the coast road—Cally staring helplessly at her puffy eyes and red cheeks in the wing mirror—he rolled the car to a standstill outside a modern white building just on the outskirts of the main town.

'Where are we?'

Leon unfolded his lithe frame from the seat beside her and walked round to open her door. 'That day when you called the university and I wasn't there—I was here.'

Cally sighed. Four months ago, she had wanted nothing more than for him to show her where he had been all those mornings. Now it just seemed too little, too late. 'You don't need to show me.'

'Yes, I do.'

Reluctantly, Cally followed him round to the front of the elegant building. He swiped a card and led them inside. It smelled of fresh paint, and there were workmen's tools scattered on the floor.

'This part should be finished by the end of the week,' he said. 'The rest is complete.'

Stepping over plastic sheeting, he led her through to an enormous atrium, and that was when she saw them. There, on the wall in front of her, were the Rénards, flanked by enormous windows which looked out over the Mediterranean.

Cally immediately hurried closer, her mind suddenly oblivious to everything except the ingenious way in which they'd been displayed. 'His love by the sea,' she whispered in disbelief, her eyes darting between the paintings and the view, then falling to the beautifully presented accompanying details which gave information on their composition and credited her with the restoration work. 'When, how— What is this place?'

'Ever since my mother told me I was descended from a

great painter, it occurred to me that Montéz was lacking its own art gallery.' Leon shrugged, as if it had ceased to matter now. 'Once I started working with Professeur Lefevre, I realised that the students at the university were going to need somewhere to showcase their own work too. So I started to have this place built. I just hadn't planned to tell anyone until it was completely finished.'

'It's perfect,' Cally said slowly, the genius of it running through her mind. 'The big names will draw hundreds of visitors, and the students' work will immediately be in the public eye.' She shook her head in wonder. 'Do you mean to tell me that you planned to display the Rénards here all along?'

Leon ran a hand over his forearm uncomfortably. 'Much as I would like to say yes, that was not my intention initially. I bought that Goya in London, amongst others, to display here. But I bought the Rénards for myself. I suppose I wanted a little of *my* father's history inside the palace.' His eyes lifted to meet hers. 'Until you made me realise that if I kept them there I would have more in common with that tyrannical sixteenth-century king than with my own ancestors.'

'If I had known why you wanted them I would never have been so tactless,' she said regretfully.

'But, like you said, the blood that runs through my veins ought to be irrelevant. They deserve to be enjoyed by everyone. Besides, when it came down to it, they were not as hard to part with as something else.' Leon nodded to the wall behind her and she turned.

'My painting!' Cally cried, utterly overwhelmed, and yet also wholly embarrassed to see her landscape, beautifully framed, hanging just a few feet away from the

Rénards. An enormous lump rose in her throat that she had a job to swallow. 'I—I thought if you found it you'd throw it in the sea.'

Leon shook his head. 'It's brilliant, Cally.'

'Hardly.'

Leon raised his eyebrows. She looked at it again, and was forced to concede that it didn't look as dire as she had imagined it might. Not that she had ever expected to see it again.

'I thought you didn't do your own work.'

'I hadn't done.' She shook her head. 'Ever since David. But then I met you.'

She could admit that now—that her inspiration, which had disappeared in Paris, hadn't risen again in Montéz because she'd been in a new and exciting part of the world but because being with the man she loved had been stimulating in every way there was. And constantly surprising, she thought, as seeds of hope dared to take root in her mind.

He nodded and looked up at it. 'I mean it when I say it's brilliant. When I look at it, it's like I can actually feel the passion you felt when you painted it.'

Cally blushed. 'There's probably a reason for that'.

Leon shook his head. 'No, I don't just mean *that*. It's like it's alive with your excitement for the strokes themselves, the colours, the sheer joy of painting.'

Cally drew in a sharp breath and felt the most acutely powerful tears she had ever known prick behind her eyes. He hadn't laughed or tossed it out to sea, wasn't suggesting that her love of painting buried an ulterior motive, nor had he once even implied that a girl like her should never harbour dreams about becoming an artist. He'd framed it, treasured it and hung it in a gallery beside the paintings which had fired her love of art in the first place. 'Thank you,' she said suddenly, her emotions threatening to overwhelm her. 'For understanding what it means to me. I thought—'

'That I'd always presume your career was just something to fill your time until you married? I know,' he said flinchingly. 'You'd think that with everything you endured in order to work on the Rénards I ought to have realised earlier.'

Cally drew in a very deep breath, and for a moment it felt like the world had stopped spinning. All this time she'd been convinced that he saw no need to let her in because he had no desire to understand her... And all the while he had understood her better than anyone she had ever met. She stared at him in utter amazement. 'It wasn't as hard to endure as you might think,' she whispered.

Leon didn't seem to hear her. 'I should have brought you here earlier,' he said hopelessly. 'There are a lot of things I should have done earlier. But this I had planned to tell you...at our wedding. I was just waiting for Jen to let me know whether she could make the date I'd fixed for the grand opening.'

Cally stared at him, dumbfounded by this new information. 'Jen?' Her *sister* Jen?

'I've invited her to cover the story. I'd planned to invite Kaliq and Tamara too,' he continued with immense effort. 'Maybe it isn't the only thing I should think about revealing to the public.'

As she looked up into his face, lined as it was with anguish, full of strength, that was the moment when she knew that everything was going to be OK. Because she suddenly understood that he hadn't just chosen to keep his guard up when he was around *her,* but that ever since childhood he had been forced to keep the truth a secret from everyone. But he was trying to change, and it was because of her.

'That's fantastic,' she whispered, her heartbeat beginning to pound in her ears.

Leon shrugged, his whole pose listless. 'I know that displaying the paintings can't undo all the wrong I've done you, but I just… I need you to understand that you have shaped the way I feel about everything. There were a hundred practical reasons that I held responsible for my proposal to you, but the truth is that I would have dismissed them all if you hadn't changed the way I feel about marriage altogether. That month we spent here together— it was the best of my life.'

He took a deep breath. 'I know I can't ask that of you now, but, if you meant it when you said that you loved me, then please let me learn how to love you properly, how to love our son properly.'

Cally felt a warm glow begin to flow through her, like a diver catching sight of the mast of a sunken ship he had given up hope of ever finding. For those were the words which confirmed that unearthing the rest of Leon's heart was going to be the easy part. 'Something tells me that now you've set your mind to it you're going to be a fast learner.' She smiled.

Leon looked at her in awe, feeling the tension in his shoulders begin to seep away, wondering if he dared let it. 'I don't care how long it takes.'

Cally squeezed his hand and fleetingly she thought she saw him blink back a tear. It was a gesture which confirmed that he understood how close they had both come to losing something so precious, that he was happy to take things slowly, and above all that she could trust him. With it, she was struck by the most phenomenal moment of fulfilment she had ever known.

Well, emotionally speaking, Cally thought with a grin, as she ran her eyes over his impossibly handsome face and athletic body, as drop-dead gorgeous today as he had been that night in London…and every night since.

'As long as it takes,' she repeated thoughtfully. 'But, you know, you have taught me the benefits of acting impulsively, giving in to what *feels* right.' Her eyes gleamed wickedly.

Leon took a cautious step towards her, his tone husky. 'What are you saying, *ma belle?*'

'The church is booked for four days from now, is it not?'

He looked at her in amazement and shook his head in joyous disbelief. 'You mean you want to go ahead with the wedding, just as we planned?'

Cally beamed, thinking how far he had come, how far they had both come. 'Unless you think that is a little *too* rash?'

Leon shook his head commandingly and pulled her close. '*Non, mon amour par la mer,*' he whispered. 'I think that would make me the happiest man alive.'

* * * * *

"YOU HAVE MADE him proud," he told her, nodding at her father, feeling benevolent. "You are the jewel of his kingdom."

Finally, she turned her head and met his gaze, her sea-colored eyes were clear and grave as she regarded him.

"Some jewels are prized for their sentimental value," she said, her musical voice pitched low, but not low enough to hide the faint tremor in it. "And others for their monetary value."

"You are invaluable," he told her, assuming that would be the end of it. Didn't women love such compliments? He'd never bothered to give them before. But Gabrielle shrugged, her mouth tightening.

"Who is to say what my father values?" she asked, her light tone unconvincing. "I would be the last to know."

"But I know," he said.

"Yes." Again, that grave, sea-green gaze. "I am invaluable, a jewel without price." She looked away. "And yet, somehow, contracts were drawn up, a price agreed upon and here we are."

There was the taint of bitterness to her words then. Luc frowned. He should not have indulged her—he regretted the impulse. This was what happened when emotions were given reign.

"Tell me, princess," he said, leaning close, enjoying the way her eyes widened, though she did not back away from him. He liked her show of courage, but he wanted to make his point perfectly clear. "What was your expectation? Do not speak to me of contracts and prices in this way, as if you are the victim of some subterfuge," he ordered her, harshly. "You insult us both."

Her gaze flew to his, and he read the crackling temper there. It intrigued him as much as it annoyed him—but either way he could not allow it. There could be no rebellion, no bitterness, no intrigue in this marriage. There could only be his will and her surrender.

He remembered where they were only because the band chose that moment to begin playing. He sat back in his chair, away from her. *She is not merely a business acquisition,* he told himself, once more grappling with the urge to protect her—safeguard her. *She is not a hotel, or a company.*

She was his wife. He could allow her more leeway than he would allow the other things he controlled. At least today.

"No more of this," he said, rising to his feet. She looked at him warily. He extended his hand to her and smiled. He could be charming if he chose. "I believe it is time for me to dance with my wife."

Indulge yourself with this passionate love story that starts out as a royal marriage of convenience, and look out for more dramatic books from Caitlin Crews and Harlequin Presents in 2010!

HARLEQUIN *Presents*

PREGNANT BRIDES

Inexperienced and expecting,
they're forced to marry!

Bestselling Harlequin Presents author

Lynne Graham

brings you the second story
in this exciting new trilogy:

RUTHLESS MAGNATE,
CONVENIENT WIFE
#2892
Available February 2010

Also look for

GREEK TYCOON,
INEXPERIENCED MISTRESS
#2900
Available March 2010